Also by Jack Tyler Jones

Vice and Virtue

Adam at the End of the World

Tumbling Through Eternity

The Island of Killing Tourists

The Kingdom of Smoke and Mushrooms

For Kelcey,

and for Nick.

Featuring cover art by Laura DuBose.

Kelkee

Just so you know what I've been thinking,
when you sail and when you're sinking,
when you laugh and sing the blues,
you're going to be the one I choose.

I'll take your smiles and your tears;
I'll take your courage and your fears,
and everything that you dish out
will be what I will care about.

I accept you, soul and skin,
who you are and who you've been,
who you hate and who you love,
and who you'll be when someday comes.

When you're a saint and when you sin,
you're still my love; you're still my friend,
and still I'll want you (it's my choice)
when you scream and lose your voice,
when you heal and when you bleed,
when you want and when you need,
when you cling and when you shove,
I'll love you all of the above.

When you're joyful, when you're sad,
when you've gone stark raving mad,
when you've torn yourself to shreds,
I'm going to do what Samwise said:
I cannot take the load from you,
but what I can, I'll surely do -
I'll bundle you up on my back,
and carry you up the lonely track
of wilderness and desolation.
I'll love you in your desecration.

And when you're near and when you're far,
in burning sun or freezing stars,
I'm with you each mistake and scar.
I love you just the way you are.

To Put Your Tears In My Eyes

My heart is a con artist

creeping through his streets

carrying old bullets

coat tattered around shoulders

drooping beneath weight

drowning in rain and sorrow

drenched in anticipation

each time he paces my mind

each footfall echoing

every call his number

gravity of my hope

inside out

just put me out of my

just put me out of my

zeal for his every move.

"Ah, shut up, Bowie." – David Bowie, Berlin, 2002

Yes, well, there were some things I never told David Bowie, things that happened between his death and me finding you. Choices that I had to make alone. That's why I'm eager to speak with you, Mr. Jones. Exulansis. I thought we could begin with the incident where I killed my baby, but then I thought: we all could use a bit of context.

The creature was composing one of its lists.

The first time I met David Bowie, he was the Goblin King. I was about to be in kindergarten, and Scarlet was soon to enter first grade. It was ladies' cocktail night, and our mother's turn to hostess. We were the only children there, inevitable, it being our house, all other children relegated to other adults in other households from six to ten pm. Our mother did not actually drink. She only hosted those who did, presiding over their gabblings and displays. Our father was somewhere around.

Scarlet and I were shut out of sight and out of sound in the den. The ladies were down the hall, in the dining room. They were all worked up, laughing and jabbering, grasping each other by this or that arm, gasping, tears of mixed emotions tracing canyons in foundation on their cheeks, dropping off the cliffs of their jaws, or more likely, being smeared away on a crimson-colored paper napkin before they got that far.

We were allowed to watch what we wanted on tv that night, and eat ice cream and popcorn for dinner. The den was dim, lots of reds and browns. It was maybe August. School hadn't started yet. I'd been quiet that summer, after my year at God's Promise Nursery School. Scarlet and I watched Labyrinth. It was my first time seeing it. It was not a matter of how the film portrayed the Goblin King. My mind only needed an image to attach to a persona of its own. A fingerpainting to go on the page.

By that point, I already considered myself to be two. My parents named me Anne Elizabeth Scarborough, like the fair, and called me Annieliz. My sister was Aubri Scarlet Scarborough, like the song, who went by Scarlet, and from birth had flowing hair, with the colors and swirliness of a stormy beach. Scarlet was only one, as far as I knew.

I'm only one person, and I knew it then, but I was also two, in my mind; the two of us, little girls of four and a half, were in our head. One turned five, then six. Seven. She held the hand of her little friend. As I grew up and grew older, I saw myself inwardly as my present age, and holding my four-year-old me on one hip or the other, in my arms. That particular bit had never been able to grow up. It had been broken in the banana room.

Lotion, toothpaste, sourdough bread.

It was the Goblin King who put it to us that I could save ourself a lot of heartache by saying that I was allergic to bananas. It's an emotional allergy, the Goblin King said. It's not a lie. He was wearing his blue and purple sparkly getup, with the moon necklace. His hair was like the residue in the air after a firecracker.

God's Promise Nursery School was run by the Sharons. Smoking Sharon and Non-smoking Sharon. Smoking Sharon went outside a lot. She was there every day except for Tuesdays and Thursdays. Non-smoking Sharon was older, and she was the one who let us get borrowed at naptime.

Lemonade.

The mention of naps or sleeping gives me a spooky feeling, like right before a tornado. I know that they weren't really bananas. Anne-me understands what Elizabeth-me was unable to comprehend at the time. Yellow condoms, on, look like bananas in their peels. The tips, the texture, the irregularities of color showing through from the men's skins underneath. And peels come off. And inside, there is goo. Latex makes me shiver. But bananas, when they get too close, make me cry.

There was a toy octopus in the banana room, one of the basement classrooms of the Methodist church that played host to God's Promise Nursery School. At naptime, sometimes, when Smoking Sharon wasn't there, the man who I would come to think of as Frank Ferlinghetti would meet us at the top of the stairs. When we went down there, usually one of us at a time, some of the children never, some of the children often, and I was often, the friends of Frank Ferlinghetti would be seated in the metal folding chairs, around the card table.

The man who would loom in my mind for years loomed above me then, black hair shining, large nose like a pirate, big, straight teeth. He said, Let's pretend like we're making a movie.

The octopus watched.

I had nightmares about bananas. People coming near me with them. That was what the bad men were hurting me with, bananas, as far as I knew. When Anne-me started to grow up, and figure this out, Elizabeth-me knew it, too. But I still feel the same way, and I still have nightmares about bananas. Scarlet caught on to this fear, and loved to chase me around the house with them, telling me that the bananas would eat me. She tried the same with apples, creating a temporary phobia, but it didn't stick. The Goblin King thought it was silly, though apples still give us a vaguely uncomfortable feeling, like we're about to get bitten.

When I woke up from banana nightmares, if it was still the middle of the night, sometimes I'd lie awake and travel in my mind to the Castle Bowie. I found my way there, to the Goblin King.

It was, on the outside, the size of a large manor house, but with dark brown and greyish-black stones and bricks, towers and turrets, a drawbridge. It loomed in the thick silver air, on the brink of a storm. There was a moat, if I wanted there to be a moat.

I knew that the Goblin King was played by an actor, of course, who turned out to be a singer, and so on. It was the Goblin King who put forth the idea of having a council inside the castle, and it was the Goblin King who was the first member. He helped Anne-me learn how to take care of Elizabeth-me, though as it turned out, Elizabeth-me was good at many things that Anne-me struggled to accomplish.

Elizabeth was instinct. Elizabeth was a microscope and a telescope playing pattycake. Elizabeth was the first to wake up. She was right-handed, and Anne was left-handed, but I used my hands interchangeably. I liked school: Elizabeth liked science, while Anne preferred home ec. Our favorite movies were The Boondock Saints, and The Sword in the Stone. Our favorite show was Wilfred (even though they occasionally make rape jokes, which they absolutely should not do, since it makes rapists think that rape is not that big of a deal), which we watched at Eloise's house (Eloise has been our best friend since high school!) since she had netflix, and she also had a washing machine, and a drying machine, and they didn't even need coins. Not even Eloise, my best friend, knew that we were us inside. But it was all just me. Alone. There's only me in here, Annieliz.

The Goblin King never knew anything that I myself could not know, never came up with anything that I myself could not have said. That's how you know it's all you. If you're wondering whether God is speaking to you, or if it's just you, ask yourself: could I have thought this up on my own? If the answer is yes, then there's no need to attribute it to God.

That was the first of the Davids Bowie. Gradually, there were others. I knew about, but did not by any means immediately conjure up, various Bowies not yet exploring our inner us. They came when we needed them.

The summer immediately after high school, I once sat in the Castle Bowie for over thirty hours, plotting how to execute and dispose of the man to whom I shall refer as Frank Ferlinghetti. Anne, the Goblin King, Aladdin Sane, and Major Tom stood around the large oval table. Amber maps were scattered upon it. Six thrones were behind them.

Elizabeth was playing in a room off to the side, a room filled with cartoon animal characters based on, and bearing a striking resemblance to, the stationary printings by the name of Liza Fronk. There is a fluffy white tiger with rainbow stripes, and we communicate with our thoughts. There is a white elephant in a tuxedo and sunglasses playing a piano, a multi-colored raccoon family, even some many-colored monkeys! We love to play together, rolling around on the floor. We made our own playground, too.

So Anne and the Davids Bowie plotted to murder the only man who was always in the banana room. The others would come and go. Frank Ferlinghetti stayed.

The Thin White Duke burst in through the curtain stage right, throwing open the heavy oak door behind it. He had on black pants and a white shirt. He had on a black waistcoat, too. His hair was just so. He said, Elizabeth is thirsty.

So she was. Anne-me burst into the Liza Fronk room, and collected a weary Elizabeth-me from the side of the white-with-rainbow-stripes tiger, who looked up at Anne-me forlornly. I ran us out the gate, across the drawbridge, and down the stone path away from the brooding castle.

I stumbled into the kitchen, agog at the clock, and took three gulps from the faucet. Because three and gulp are both green to me. Then I got a glass, also a green word, and drank even more. My calves wobbled.

This must not go on, the Thin White Duke said.

The creature lacked the wits to carry out any such plot.

The Thin White Duke and I looked at Aladdin Sane and Major Tom. Major Tom's spacesuit shrugged. Aladdin Sane arched an eyebrow. The Goblin King said, Call Andy, the janitor at Scarlet's hospital.

Scarlet worked in the human resources department of the hospital down in Princeton. It wasn't the same as our hospital, which we had under the bed when we were little.

I used to get under my bed, and go down through the pink and green swirly tunnel, and Anne-me would pretend to tend to

Elizabeth-me's wounds. It was a game we played with myself. I suspect that I played it mostly on Tuesday and Thursday afternoons. But I can't be sure. It was a long time ago.

So Anne and Elizabeth looked at each other, at eye level from where I was holding me up, cuddled safely against myself. And we looked on Scarlet's laptop, and got the phone number of Andy, the janitor, who had once been called Snowbear.

I said, It's Annieliz; have you ever wanted to kill Frank Ferlinghetti?

He said, Yes, as a matter of fact, I have wanted to kill Frank Ferlinghetti; do you want to meet at Wendy's?

Wendy was not a friend of ours. It was a hamburger establishment.

Andy and I sat across from each other then. In the future, we would sit beside each other.

January 2016

We were making eye contact when Andy died. He died, the creature repeated to itself. There was an arch of blood, perhaps a gallon, drenching the fuzzy grey-ish blue seat fabric, and my body. The archway of blood was a door that I could not un-walk through. He had been holding my left hand and attempting to reassure me that I still had access to all of the things that I had once had access to. The films, the music, if not the man. Then his head was sliced off.

Minutes before, there'd been grins on our faces. We'd sung Fellowship, by Connor Grail – Having brew in the Shire! Throwing rings in the fire! - at the top of our voices, ending just as we coasted to a stop at the red light. Switched to the radio. Heard the news about David Bowie dying.

Ours was a car the color of river-covered pebbles on a late spring morning, as seen from the upswing of a rope swing, when you know that the water will be too cold to catch your breath in. His name was not Andy. He was called Andy, but his name was Snowbear; he lived his life staggering beneath the weight of his mother's pseudo-tribal, would-be-hippie phase, that is, until I came along in nursery school, and was playing with the Raggedy Anne and Andy dolls. I was called Annieliz, and he was allowed to play with me. I called him Andy, and he wore the name like a mink-lined robe, minus the suffering of minks, and that's why, from time to time up until the last time before he died, the man called Andy thanked me for saving him from becoming the man called Snowbear, except for me. I was allowed to call him either Snowbear, or Andy. Andy called me Annieliz. So did others, except doctors, and occasionally my parents, depending on volume and recent lack of rule compliance.

It was not another car that killed Andy, although we were sitting in the river pebble car when it happened, touching palms and fingers, discussing the radio's recent disclosure that David Bowie had died a few days ago, shortly after his sixty-ninth birthday (I found that to be fitting, since both my six and my nine are red, and he wore red makeup prominently as Aladdin Sane), shortly after the release of his latest album, which I hadn't even bought yet; we were going to maybe go and get it that afternoon, since we'd just had Martha put down at the vet - God rest her soul - but not now, not so soon after the announcement; I just wanted to get home and get some rest, since I was pregnant, and then Andy sneezed, so I said, May the force be ever in your favor, but rather a bunch of windows. A bunch of windows killed Andy. They flew off the back of a window truck, and hit Andy where he sat, entirely un-duck-like. His spine was twisted, at first because he was turned toward me at the red light, chatting, and then because it had been severed and mangled by a large metal and glass rectangle. His head bounced off the passenger-side window with a smear and landed in my lap.

Martha was my pug. I had had her since I was fifteen years old; I was, and the time of the three deaths - David Bowie, Martha, and Andy, in both chronological and order of least importance - twenty-nine years old. Martha had been a faithful pug, waddling and wrinkling at me in all of her guileless, bug-eyed befuddlement. Andy and I were driving back from the vet when the windows decapitated him, punctured him, and otherwise made him not exist any longer.

There was no such thing as Andy anymore. There was no such thing as Martha. There was not, in the Andy and Martha sense, any such thing as David Bowie. The things that had once been David Bowie were now other things - atoms drifting apart, reconfiguring.

There I was climbing out of the car. How could the radio still be on? His head, hair tangled in the fingers of my right hand, dangled near my thighs. His right arm, not attached to the rest of his body, was held in my left hand. I did not know which to let go of in order to call 911. Someone else did, eventually. I was still standing by the remains of the car as the sky and the car's paint began to match with the imminence of rain. My body was making a low howling noise, and my torso repeatedly convulsed. Perhaps four or perhaps five cars had been stopped by the wreckage. My body continued to make the noise, more gulping now. There was snot. There was spit. I still hadn't let go of Andy's body parts. The things that had once contained Andy, the parts that had mattered most, were in his head. But they weren't there anymore. The electricity had gone out from behind his eyes. No one came near me, until an ambulance arrived. They stood off at a distance, with hands over mouths and arms over stomachs. The lights and sirens hurt me. Ape creatures pried the bits of carbon that used to be Andy Snowbear from my confused and taken aback fingers. I stared at the paramedics, knowing what they were, but unable to decipher the expressions playing upon their faces.

Days later, when I sat in my best friend's diner, Chez Eloise, on a red vinyl stool with silver – it was that kind of place, lots of red and silver, and a black and white checked floor, and a jukebox, and a long window where you could watch the cook cooking your meal - which is what I was doing, watching Eugene, he had the same sort of look on his face as those paramedics had.

I had loved Andy with every individual part of my being, and with all of it together. He had smoked cigarettes, but I never made a peep about it. He never littered. Andy was a big boy. But Andy did not exist anymore. Windows are better than cancer, I reasoned. Even in dying early, because I had learned to do it, I could love Andy. Andy did not exist anymore, but I had learned how to love him. In the presence of his death, I could learn how to love Eugene, if we wanted. He was busy living a life full of joys and triumphs that we knew nothing about, and stresses, stresses, stresses that maybe we could help to relieve. We could learn how to celebrate with him, and comfort him, if he wanted. He didn't.

In the cooking window, doing the cooking, was the long figure, blond at the fur. We had gone to community college together. We'd known each other a little before then, at his church, and at the nursing home volunteer nights where Andy and I later did our puppet shows. We sometimes shared a table with Eloise and other apes at open mic poetry nights down in Princeton, but he never gave a reading. We had played chess. He thought he was something else. Eugene vs. Annieliz chess games were predictable; he'd win almost all of the time. He took his losses as my luck, not even having the humility to suspect himself of having an off day. But here was the true case: sometimes Anne let Elizabeth play by herself. It was scary, because it's nearly impossible for a four-year-old to pass herself off as an adult, even when she's living out of an adult body. But she won every single time, every time that she played alone. We were smug, but secretly.

I could also win if I used the combined powers of the Davids Bowie. Eugene never knew what hit him, but he never needed to know. He said one time, I've never met a woman who was smarter than me. All I said was, I'm sure there are some, but it made me like him less. It made him less attractive. He thought that he was smarter than all of the women he'd ever met, and he didn't mind saying so – to a woman. What a cad. (But a foxy cad, Anne.) I felt surges of pity for him, because it obviously wasn't true. He and we both knew women who were smarter than he was, if that's how you wanted to think of it, but that's not how you have to think of it. Everyone knows things that you don't. Everyone has been to places, inside or outside of their bodies, where you have never been. You have something to learn from everybody. I tried hard to maintain my respect for him. It took effort.

But on the other hand, I could see myself being his 1950s housewife, vacuuming in pearls, an apron, and nothing. He'd been useful to me, in the time we'd known each other – a person with whom to engage in affectionate chatter, a person who tolerated my innumerable spasms of awkwardness, a person who, if he overestimated himself, at least also sought to see the big and the bright in other people. That much could be said, that if he was full of himself, he was also full of those around him. I liked him, how he held my hand during a few weeks of the first state park summer, when Andy and I were not together. I liked how Eugene asked before he hugged me. No surprises. Usually.

His face was droopy, like melted wax. He had a beard long enough for me to find it incongruous with his buzz cut; neither good nor bad, but aesthetically strange to me, like a skinny person named Bertha (sorry, skinny people named Bertha). He wore glasses, sometimes the hot pair, and sometimes the regular pair. I wondered why he didn't wear the hot pair more often. I also wondered why he didn't have the hot haircut more often, instead of keeping it that short. But we knew that it was not our place to question him.

Eugene was making us breakfast. Tears came out of our eyes when he made comments like, You're going to eat all of that? He hurt Elizabeth's feelings. I left my food all on the plate and stared at him for as long as it would have taken me to eat it, mouth closed, tension gathered at my temples, leaving it untouched. I still tipped Penny or Peggy, though.

Eugene looked at Annieliz on her cherry bar stool with her orange juice and her pinot noir mouth from his ensconcement in the kitchen window.

I usually went ahead and ate in front of him though, remembering what the Goblin King had taught us about power – that he had no power over us. The fact was, Eugene was a pedant. He tried to assume places that we had not given him. I wondered what he looked like to other people. I sometimes thought him handsome. He might be ugly. We couldn't be sure.

I examined my desire for him. It was not a desire to win his approval to assure myself of my place in the tribe, under his protection, respect in exchange for inclusion, that sort of thing. I think it was more biological than that; my body thought his body would probably be a suitable match with which to make other bodies. Bodies to play out similar bodily functions as these - sex, birth - until the planet burned out the virus. Why, please.

Eugene prepared scrambled eggs with cheeses of various kinds, and a pancake. Penny or Peggy refilled my orange juice. Eloise leaned across the counter toward me. That one, she said. I nodded. It was Giovanni Mockingbird. We had so many questions.

An apology is an act of submission. That's what I wanted. Because one day, he'd scared me, Eugene. With the way he'd hugged me, and much moreso, the way he didn't apologize when I let him know that he'd made us uncomfortable. I'd taken the courage to stand up for myself, and for what? Nothing. A loss of friendship. And still, I was haunted by that hug. He'd asked if he could have a hug, but then when I'd nodded, he'd given me a side hug, which I wasn't expecting. I couldn't ignore him, because he put the lyrics back in the music. But I hate feeling pressured, trapped, cornered like that. And there had been people around; I hate being watched. It was just like Shaggy the Wizard, who I'll tell you about in a minute, a body all sideways, touching me along the side of my body, all down me, so that I could feel the redness of his wizardry, and it made me sad. The thought thought its way through me and wouldn't be unthought until Eugene had either apologized, or I'd at least done my best to let him know how I felt. I felt uncomfortable around him, afraid, unsure, unsafe. So I used my cumbersome flip phone to send him a text message, even though I hate text messaging, because I was too afraid to face him, because he scared me. I told him that it was eating me up, that I didn't want to be afraid of him. He didn't answer with a text, or a call, or a carrier pigeon. It was the same as when we'd had plans to have lunch together one day, and he simply never showed up, then acted like nothing was wrong the next time we ran into him. But perhaps he'd never received the text about the scary hug, so I tried leaving a note for him with Eloise. Still nothing. I still went to Chez Eloise. Sometimes, I even still ate his cooking. But I felt a thrill of revulsion when I looked at Eugene now, like a Cro-Magnon looking at a Neanderthal. He wouldn't bow his head to me about anything big, the way he would if he'd stepped on my foot. I tried not to mythologize it, the bad hug. But I couldn't stop crinkling my nose around him; his bad manners were smelly, and the way he expressed his insecurities by acting pompous came at me with all the repugnance and pity I felt for a caught fish. I'd still eat the fish, though, if I were starving, or maybe even if I wasn't: it was already dead, after all. I wanted Eugene to make it go away. He had the power to. He could evolve, become the type of person who cares how his bodily presence in other people's space impacts them emotionally. I appreciated him for cooking me breakfast at dinner time, even though that was his job, as the cook at a breakfast-for-dinner diner. They didn't call it that. But anyway, I realized that Eugene and I didn't have to be friends. Perhaps we had been friends once, in community college, playing chess, holding hands. But I don't have to be friends with someone who makes me feel afraid.

Eugene could be anus-mouthed at times. I hated it when he did it to me, but I won't deceive you: it was amusing to see it done to others. Wrong, but amusing things sometimes are. He shouldn't have done it, and I'm not saying that it was ok, but Elizabeth might have laughed when this woman complained that her bacon was cold, and Eugene replied from inside of his window that in any case, if her eyes were any further apart, she'd be an herbivore. Eloise gave the lady her money back. Another time when Eloise had to give somebody's money back was when the wrong plate got handed to this lady. She was served a man wearing plaid's eggs with ketchup. Normally, people put their own ketchup on, but this guy had arthritis, bad, and he was a regular, and this lady wasn't, and it was Penny or Peggy who put the wrong plate down, and Eloise is too nice to fire her, even though she always makes mistakes. So the lady with the man's ketchup covered eggs scowled at Penny or Peggy, and said, What is this? Eugene, from his window, said, Your mom's abortion. Anne, overhearing, put her hand over her heart, held her breath, and looked down past her orange juice, past her cherry barstool, past the black and white floor. I laughed, though.

I still allowed myself some Eugene fantasies, from time to time, despite all things. I often thought of him holding me, in the days since Andy died.

Ok, eggs, frozen breadsticks, frozen pizza - thin crust, so we can fold it!

Andy and I were at Wendy's, discussing our mutual interest in the downfall of the one called Frank Ferlinghetti. Frank Ferlinghetti had a wizard, a man I think of as Shaggy, because he looked like the cartoon. I know he wasn't really a wizard, but he might as well have been. How is a four-year-old supposed to distinguish between real and fake wizards? He had a wand and a red robe and a red pointy hat and an amulet and everything. I believed what grownups said; it's what they were for. How was the me who would remain Elizabeth supposed to know? He cast a spell, upon me and almost certainly upon the others, or so we understood him to do. A spell so that we wouldn't be able to talk about what happened in the banana room. And as far as I knew, no one ever had. But Andy, I knew why he'd played out scenarios in his mind, revenge scenarios. We did not ask each other. We told as far as we needed to tell, eating our chicken sandwiches, across from each other.

Andy and I decided that it'd be best to put aside the matter of Frank Ferlinghetti, for the present moment at least. We could revisit the subject as needed, but one mustn't obsess, as the Thin White Duke was wont to say.

That was the first day I'd ever seen him, the Thin White Duke, the day that Andy and I decided to put aside the hypothetical murder of the one called Frank Ferlinghetti.

Andy and I got a different goal together. The Thin White Duke and the others and I stood around the oval table with the maps, and he said, why don't you see if Andy wants to go to all of the state parks in West Virginia?

And Andy did.

It was a bucket list thing, although it didn't need to be. I had a cyst on my brain, in my cerebellum. The Yellowstone caldera of my body, it could blow at any time. I called the cyst Harold. Like a herald of doom. Or perhaps the cyst called itself Harold. We couldn't be sure. Death loomed, slightly. So Andy and I began to make lists of nearby and further-off parks to visit, thirty-six in all, plus two rail lines.

Four days later we drove down to Chief Logan and hiked without speaking. Throughout the next few years of our relationship, whenever we were going through something big, the way other people say to sleep on it, we'd ask each other, Do you want to go hiking about that? And later added, Do you want to have sex about that? We solved a lot of problems with our physical activities. We got married at the courthouse, just us and our parents and Scarlet and a judge, shortly after we found out that we were going to have a baby. Andy said that he wanted to make things official, to set things in order. He did. More than I knew.

Each evening, after our walk around the trailer park, Andy got his choice of a back rub or a foot rub. I usually went to the castle to read with the Davids Bowie while our body massaged him. One Saturday evening, after our monthly volunteer night doing a puppet show at the nursing home, I was sitting on Andy's butt, kneading his shoulders, while skiing the big mountain with Ziggy Stardust and the Thin White Duke. When we got back down to the castle, we had hot chocolate by the fire, and they read me a story.

It was a story about a man in fat prison, exercising to pay off this workout debt. The other prisoners had started laughing, and they hadn't stopped laughing. Soon, most of the guards had it, too. One of the ones who wasn't laughing let the fat man out, and he told the fat man not to read anything that a laughing person showed him.

The man went outside of the prison. He was still fat. The whole world was laughing, but not at him. The laughing people, with their eyes shining, would go up to non-laughers, and show them scraps of paper. The non-laughers, after reading, began laughing. Anyone who laughed at what was written on the paper would never stop laughing again, until he was taken by death.

Laughing people died of dehydration and heart attacks, to be buried by others who could do nothing that could not be done while also laughing. They died of exhaustion by the millions, for few could sleep while laughing. Everyone who wasn't laughing yet was reduced to prey being hunted by those who wanted to share the joke, or whatever it was, on the scraps of paper. Reading was a hazard; it soon became illegal, in an effort to try and stop the spread of the plague.

As fewer and fewer non-laughing humans remained, even mass burials were rendered impractical. And some of the laughers had gained the power of speech. For a week, the only word that any of them said was The. Then, as time progressed, through the gales of laughter, more and more words started breaking through, always in the same order. The, they said. The. The. The. The Meaning. The Meaning. The Meaning. The Meaning. On and on they laughed, grabbing people by the arms, doubling over, grinning madly into the horrified faces of those they had once loved. The Meaning Of. The Meaning Of. Thousands of attempts were made by each and every laugher to spread the message verbally, now that the non-laughing population had gone to extreme measures to avoid reading the joke. A few had blinded themselves deliberately, in order to save themselves from laughing to death. But what would they do, once the joke could be spread by word of mouth?

The Meaning Of Life. The Meaning Of Life. The Meaning Of Life.

Finally, the whole world was laughing, except for that one fat guy, who was not so fat anymore, since he'd been running, and hiding, and hardly able to eat anything, so consumed was he in trying to escape the millions of insistent, wandering laughers.

The Meaning Of Life Is. The Meaning Of Life Is.

The Meaning Of Life Is.

The fat man was backed into a corner, a laughing man with a maniacal gleam in his eyes lurching toward him with jerky, too-long-in-the-desert steps. The Meaning Of Life Is.

The formerly fat man stuck a hand gun in his own mouth, and fired it, never to laugh again.

Ziggy Stardust closed the book on his lap and said, They were wrong about the meaning of life, though, the people with the joke. Perhaps if they'd known, they'd have been able to stop laughing.

I said, What is the meaning of life, then?

The Thin White Duke said, The meaning of life is hooting back at owls.

Andy sat up. He'd been lying quietly on the living room floor of the trailer, enjoying his post-massage feelings of bliss, as I drew in my daily sketch journal.

What's that you've got there, Littlebear? he said.

He knew that I made at least one drawing per day, but he didn't necessarily know that they were drawings of the day I happened to be having, since they tended to be fantastical landscapes filled with neon animals and rock star personas, sprinkled in with incarnations of my toys and manifestations of David Bowie's stories.

I showed Andy the picture, and his eyebrows huddled together for warmth.

Cake mix. A can of frosting. Cupcake papers.

Late one June night, when our baby was four months old, and Andy was five months dead, my thoughts swirled in to the shape of Eugene. I wanted to crack like an egg in his arms, and sob for the relief in it, gasping and snotting as he held me about everything that had happened since shortly before Jaimie Taylor was born. But he was a potato without butter or salt – functional, nourishing, and mean. He was stingy with his part in the friendship we were making. Like two people knitting a sweater. Maybe he didn't want to be friends after all. I couldn't let down my guard around him enough to fully engage with him, even in my improbable fantasies. When I pictured him holding me, I was interrupted by memories of times he'd been mean to me and never apologized. A blanket apology would do, recognizing his tendency to speak barbs, and promising to be more careful in the future. But if Eugene was the self-reflective, aware-of-impact sort of man who would be responsible enough to engage with other people about their deep feelings, I hadn't seen it yet. And in any event, he had not offered.

My thoughts turned to Andy. I lay with my panties scrunched down around my thighs, and bade my fingers to dance their tribal rhythms, rhythms that would call for an appearance of their god. I felt an orgasm prowling through my guts like a beast, rumbling as it searched for an opportunity to break free. The baby wailed. It would

surely be nothing that could not wait an additional ninety seconds –
eating or its opposite – but I did not wait the additional ninety
seconds. I slung my legs out from under the covers, yanking my
panties back up with one hand as I teetered slightly on my way
across the hall, toward her crib, toward her screams.

Though, she was no longer screaming. The room was
shadowed, but I could see well enough. The yellow blanket that
Andy and I had chosen, purchased, and put into the crib, was on
top of our child's face, freakishly tight, like a plaster of Paris cast. I
reached out and yanked the cloth away from her face. Elizabeth
smiled; this was her move, mainly, as the creature of instinct. Save
the young. They have potential.

But what exactly that potential might be was another
question. I had understood, by now, that I had been wrong to have
a child, that it had been a mistake made due to flaws in my own
personality. But I had accepted responsibility. I was a parent by my
own doing. But Jaimie Taylor was a child through no fault of her
own. And children, as we know, suffer.

In the creation of Jaimie Taylor, I had brought about potential joy, but guaranteed suffering. A childhood without a father, for starters. The crying had resumed beneath me as I stood over her crib. She was suffering now, as she had since the day she was born, crying, wailing before my attempts to comfort and placate her. And why not? What monster was I, to have rolled the dice for her, knowing that the options this world had on offer included the banana room? How could I have brought her here, knowing that we would be parted, by death if not before? Knowing that the children of good, watchful parents still wind up in the clutches of unrelenting evil. I was wrong, and I was sorry. I was sorry that I had created a little ball of suffering, and destined it to grow up in a crowded, complicated world, doomed to struggle to feed and shelter herself, shackled with bills and obligations unasked for. A world in which there was no sure way to dodge rapists, in which starvation and disease were already rampant. A world which was headed for disasters of climate and artificial intelligence. The bloated population would burst. The dregs of society would hunt in packs for food, divide into violent gangs, dominate and enslave in the absence of leaders who could maintain agriculture and distribution of grid resources. The world that I had grown up in was bad; it was a world where men like Frank Ferlinghetti were powerful, and sure of their power. But the world that Jaimie Taylor would grow up in would be the world of The Hive, and there was no telling what the factions might do, how they might unify, and worse, engage each other in mind-to-mind warfare through the internet. Virtual reality, now a thing of video games, will be sophisticated torture devices of corrupt authorities by the time Jaimie Taylor would be old enough to commit a crime. And what about that? Suppose that Jaime Taylor grew up to be evil. Hitler had a mom, and I bet that she loved him.

And for what? So that she could grow up to be a good woman, striving and spending to be aesthetically pleasing to the men around her who were physically more imposing, for long enough to entice one into impregnating her, rending her body, producing children over whom to then spend decades passive-aggressively dominating? She could make other choices. She could be big. She could be great. But she'd probably be average. Grow up and go or not go to community college, work in a store, or perhaps become a nurse, to help when human bodies suck, or an astronaut, to find a new planet for humans to live on, since they've been so expedient about annihilating this one. She'd probably be no smarter, no kinder, no more special than anyone else. I wasn't, and neither were most of the people I knew. People sucked; even the ones I liked were a Swiss cheese of unpredictability. They had moods, the humans. They had opinions. And most of the time, they were wrong. About most things, too, they were wrong. Jaimie Taylor would have to learn everything for the first time, like a caveman. This is fire. Fire is hot. Hot burns. Burns hurt. Hurt kills. You're going to die anyway.

It was pointless, but did there need to be a point? She could carry on as usual, as I had, more or less having a good time, if not accomplishing anything widely notable. Was existence itself so bad? But for me, it had been. Childhood was something that I just didn't want to put a child through. And I should have thought about that before: that when you create a child, you also create a childhood. And it may not be a happy one; it may be mostly scared, like mine.

The weight of pain was simply more than the weight of pleasure. The sad things that happened took up more space than the happy things. The happies were maybies. The sads were for sure.

Anne put the yellow blanket back over the baby's face. Elizabeth turned her face into Anne's shoulder, and then looked back at the yellow outline of the face. It was the right choice. She knew this. She would go to prison with Anne, but it would be better than seeing Jaimie Taylor live in suffering any longer. Elizabeth watched in pain as the limbs of the baby flailed.

I again ran down the list of suicides. I could not leave Jaimie Taylor in this world. If I killed myself, she would end up in foster care, and kids in foster care may turn out to have lives that they feel are worthwhile, but so what? Why should I be empowered to insist that Jaimie Taylor exist in a world of suffering? That one in particular, foster care, being a world of infinite unknowns and endless changes – much like the rest of the universe. I could stay and take care of her, although I was inept, I knew. I was inadequate. Jaimie Taylor was too old to be left at a fire station;

they had closed the legal loopholes allowing anyone other than newborns to be abandoned. And abandoning her was the thing that I did not want to do, besides. I was nearly too late – but only nearly. Jaimie Taylor was just a baby, predisposed to certain things, but open to many possibilities, still. Like a puppy or a kitten, she had some personality, but was fairly generic, as beings go. She was just so new. I should have snuffed her out when she was in my womb, safe and warm, as she belonged. She was innocent. She did not deserve to live in a world that was made of places like the banana room.

I felt the silence where the Davids Bowie would have been offering each their own particular angles, testing out and discarding or adopting ideas as we deemed fit. I remembered Andy's words to me in the car, when we'd heard on the radio of David Bowie's death, right before Andy was killed, the assurance that I still had access to everything that I had once had access to. I turned toward the path, looking at the brown and grey and black distance, where the Castle Bowie stood.

But by then, Jaimie Taylor's body had quit moving. Jaimie Taylor did not exist anymore.

Elizabeth-me insisted on doing CPR. Anne-me held back from berating me; it was foolish, too late, self-contradictory, an indulgence of pseudo-remorse for an act that we all knew to be in everyone's best interests. Jaimie Taylor was dead, and that was tragic, but it was a tragedy that was always going to happen; by causing her birth, I had instigated her death, in all possible cases. I just got things going along rather sooner than they might have done, before she had to be like me, growing up in this world where the colors are too close, the beepings and the buzzings and the hummings too loud, the tags in the clothes so itchy that you can't forget the broken and despairing generationally bound sweat shop children, whittling away the bones of fingers before they're fully formed. I had spared her. But Elizabeth and Anne were doomed.

Anne-me called 911. Elizabeth-me was making a terrible racket, like a basset hound. I've killed my baby, I said to the woman who answered the telephone.

Ma'am, where are you? What is the address you are calling from? The person on the telephone did not understand. But she did not need to. The police were for that. Everyone would come. I would be the town shame, if they thought of me at all. The crazy woman who killed her baby. But I'm not crazy. We all know that. I knew what I was doing. Jaimie Taylor did not deserve the sentence of being my daughter. And so now, I would be sentenced to jail.

I called Wolfgang Savage. It was four twenty-five am.

Jaimie Taylor is gone, I said. She died.

I'll meet you at the hospital, he said.

An ambulance arrived, with its terrible wailing lights, the colors stabbing at my body, the sounds tasting of metal and cauliflower and unrinsed feet. But Jaimie Taylor didn't have to hear the overwhelming blues and reds of this world anymore. Jaimie Taylor was gone.

Elizabeth gasped from where she sat on the floor, holding the corpse of our baby. I looked up through our eyes at the paramedics who had come into the trailer of their own volition when I did not come at their knocks.

A woman in a police uniform crouched in front of me, gently touching my arm. My face had taken on a new geometry. Elizabeth looked at the woman. A paramedic was taking the baby out of my arms, off of my lap. Anne swallowed.

The yellow blanket, the policewoman said, nodding toward the crib at someone else, also dressed in blue. Maybe a paramedic, maybe a police officer. It didn't stick out to me as an important detail at the time. It wasn't. She's deduced the murder weapon already, I thought.

Glumly I admitted, I killed my baby.

The policewoman said, No.

I killed my baby, I said, voice rising in pitch, speech impediment unrelenting even in this, my most serious statement.

Tell her, the other person, also in blue, said.

You need to know, this is not an official statement, said the woman, patting my hand. The paramedics were still working on the corpse of the baby that had once been intended to grow up as Jaimie Taylor. But we all knew it was hopeless. She wasn't even the same color anymore.

The officer continued, But I feel that, given the present circumstances – your state being – that is – there's been a string of SIDS deaths, sixteen in the state of West Virginia this year, and present at all of them have been these yellow blankets. They're being recalled. There's a class action lawsuit, well, nevermind all that. What I mean is, it isn't your fault. This wasn't your doing, she said, patting my hand.

I shook my head. Tiny Atlantics and Pacifics were rounding at the tips of my eyelashes and rolling down the sloping hills of my cheeks. I would be lonely in prison. No one would want to be my friend. I didn't deserve friends, and was not capable of making any. Anne would keep our head down, and do whatever it took to protect Elizabeth.

Let's see, laundry detergent . . . library books . . .

It would have been, I reflected, the best possible time for a situation like what I'd previously had going with the Davids Bowie.

But I knew, or thought as best I could at the time and falsely concluded, that everything would go a certain way. But when had anything ever gone, even once, the way that I had thought it might? I had been accustomed to bringing all matters of significance before the Council of the Davids Bowie, and it had not been my custom to keep anything from any of us. That's why I'm so pleased to see you, Mr. Jones, and so pleased to make your acquaintance, though I admit we ran into each other at a bit of an awkward time; I was just stepping out to run errands, you see, but you knew that, obviously, and it was my choice to come to the door.

But yes, the events.

Dr. Wolfgang Savage met us at the hospital, but there was nothing that he could do. There was nothing that anyone could do. I had put an end to the life that might otherwise have played out as Jaimie Taylor.

May I give you a hug? Wolfgang Savage said, several hours later, when we were all breathing at a more steady, if still ragged, pace.

I nodded, and moved into his arms, which he opened like gates into the heaven of his torso. I stared wide-eyed past his right arm, at the wall, and the chairs, and the clock, then closed my eyes. I knew that I would want to remember the feeling, and felt shame, the imagined judgements of my fellow creatures: you cannot sit with us, you aberration. You cannot be one of the tribe. Baby killer.

But I had done right by mother nature, I knew. The planet was full. The system was overburdened. I was incapable, and unworthy. Maybe if Andy had lived, my outlook would have been different. But maybe never brought back the dead.

We're going to have to ask you a few questions, one of the people in blue said. We were at the hospital morgue. Dr. Savage had moved off to another part of the building, or perhaps the parking lot, or perhaps home. He would, days later, tell me, quietly, privately, that he could not be my gynecologist anymore. He never said why. They asked me the questions. I answered the questions. They were full before they'd even sat down to dinner. And there I'd been, gearing up to go to prison. Fully prepared to sacrifice my freedom to go outside, my freedom for Anne-me to have all of the power that Elizabeth-me had been denied, sacrificing, essentially, my most precious adulthood, by going to prison, in order to spare Jaimie Taylor from a life of pain. And they weren't even reaching for handcuffs.

Macaroni and cheese.

Halloween Jack, the bright-haired, eye-patched Bowie with the striped pants, came to me in elementary school. It was just after my friend's dad had touched me at a sleepover. Nicole knew that her dad was a kiddie-fiddler; lots of other girls in our grade knew it, too. Life's tough.

Halloween Jack held out his hands to me. He was wearing red overalls. I painted my nails that color. He was offering to hold on to certain things for me, until I was older. I had learned, in the banana room, certain things. I don't have a say. I'm not the boss. Men can do what they want. My body isn't for me. Grown-up secrets are scary. Bananas hurt to sit on. Hurting makes men breathe louder. There's no such thing as fair. You can't leave until you stop crying.

There's a hole in the bottom of the sea.

So naturally, I had questions about that, but not answers. So I handed him the questions, and he held them for me.

Halloween Jack said to me in fifth grade, you must not have that attitude of, Be perfect or I'll hate you forever. That attitude is so Old Testament.

Halloween Jack popped up to remind me any time I tried to hold something relatively small or forgivable against someone. I missed Halloween Jack, in the months after David Bowie died.

One day, Halloween Jack pointed out to me that Eugene looked a lot like my grandfather. And had a similar personality. And resembled a stickbug. I put my questions in his pockets. I wish you were mine, we thought at Eugene. I'd marry you this afternoon, since I'm going to love you to death anyway.

I wish I could keep you, Elizabeth blurted out one day, sitting by Eugene's window. He was scrambling my eggs. His eyebrows, so much like caterpillars, squirmed on his forehead. I visualized them becoming butterflies and taking off. Eugene would look weird without eyebrows.

Going about my daily life without the Davids Bowie was weird. They were a frame of reference for me, an entire way of thinking. He was everything. But, like turning off a flashlight in a lit room, I discovered that there wasn't as much difference, ultimately, as I'd have expected. But who could expect it? I'd been talking to him practically since the banana room. I knew that Andy was right. Everything that I'd ever had access to, I still had access to. The difference was in my head. But not every difference; Andy had died, and so had Martha, and so, in terms of new productions or performances, had David Bowie. I was crushed. It was heavy.

The Goblin King told me that he moved the stars for no one. He couldn't; he didn't have the power to. And neither did anyone else. He taught me to tell my memories and my past that they had no power over me. But they had power within me – he couldn't change that. I harnessed the power as best I could, channeling the way a part of me seemed to have gotten snagged and been unable to grow normally. I used it for fun, for helping me enjoy more things in more ways. I was ok with it, being two people. Plus David Bowie.

When Halloween Jack arrived – Scarlet had checked a book out from the middle school library, and he was in it, so I suppose that's how my mind got ahold of that image to imagine with – the Goblin King (he was not necessarily Jareth) proposed a council. He would share the throne room.

It could have been a council of Muppets, or a gathering of Nessie, Bigfoot, the Bunyip, and the Yeti. We considered all of these, and even trying to rope in some of the Liza Fronk animals, but in the end, I chose only the Goblin King and Halloween Jack, for the moment, to be my conspirators.

When I was older, I bought the Labyrinth books, Outside Over There, by Maurice Sendak, and Labyrinth, by A. C. H. Smith, but I haven't read them yet. Outside Over There was a children's book that I'd specifically been saving to read for the first time when Andy and I had a child of suitable age. Guess I'll read it by myself after all. Guess I'll go eat worms.

Skim milk.

The accident took place just two days after I began filling in for Scarlet as the human resources lady. Her plane left for Thailand,

and my life fell apart. It was the day of the monster truck rally, too, the demolition derby that mine and Andy's parents had been planning to go to for weeks. So they were all out of town, and I had to go to the doctor alone, as well as break the news to everyone over the phone, about Andy being removed from existence. They took it loudly.

Immediately after the accident, I had to have an OBGYN appointment, to make sure that myself and the baby were a-ok. We were.

Dr. Savage crouched by our hospital bed, twinkling.

I half rolled toward him and said, Martha's corpse. It's still in the car.

Dr. Savage cleared his throat. Ah, um, Annieliz, he started, you've been through a lot today, and.

My pug, Martha was my pug, I said. We were on our way back from the vet.

Your dog died in the accident, too? he said, looking like he'd eaten too much.

I said, No, she had organ failure. We had to have her put down.

You'd just had your dog put down? he said, his face turning into a haunted house.

Yes, I told him. Martha was gone, and then David Bowie was gone, and now Andy is gone, too. What are we going to do?

Dr. Wolfgang Savage took a deep breath and he said, We aren't going to do anything right now, Annieliz, except keep making sure that you and baby get all the care you need. Everything looks ok, though. He stood and ran a hand through the roots of his hair. He was damp with sweat. He said, I'm just so sorry that this happened to you.

I said, Nothing happened to me. They're the ones who died.

The ghosts flew out of the haunted house on his face.

Would you like a hug? he said.

I nodded, and he leaned down and shrouded my trembling shoulders with his arms. I could feel all of my expectations about life leaving me, like smoke from a wick, despite Wolfgang's attempts to hold me together.

When he uncovered me with himself, I realized that I would never get to give Martha a proper burial. My voice came out like stale bread: They'll toss out Martha's corpse when they impound the car.

You may be right, Wolfgang said, quivery-throated.

It's not fair, Elizabeth protested to Anne. They'll bring back your purse and stuff.

I know they will, I told her, stroking her hair.

I'm afraid I have to go now, Wolfgang said. A nurse will be in shortly with your paperwork.

Tylenol.

Scarlet had a happy childhood, and it still showed on her face. The one dark cloud overshadowing the whole affair was the incident with the garbage disposal, which led to her almost complete anal destruction. Scarlet Scarborough has, since the age of six, worn a prosthetic butt.

Her face – adorable upturned nose, plump pink lips, small white teeth, religiously manicured eyebrows – more than made up for the mangled meat she sat on. At least, in my opinion. Her hair fell around her shoulders and breasts like virgins into a volcano. Salivary glands were activated at the sight of her. Her long, athletic limbs, the tan, the sparkle from her makeup, the floral print clothing, like some couch from the 1970s. She could tie her laughter around men's necks and lead them about like horses, and she often did.

But she never slept with anyone. Scarlet Scarborough like the song was a virgin, waiting for marriage, and, as she put it, a boob guy.

So that's how I came about filling in for her at her job in human resources at the hospital down in Princeton for the six weeks leading up to the birth of my baby daughter. The hospital was undergoing some renovations, so her work station had been temporarily moved to the breakroom near gynecology. Not much work was getting done, and it seemed to Scarlet like the perfect time to go backpacking in Thailand for six weeks – three weeks of actual backpacking, followed by medical tourism: reconstructive butthole surgery and the subsequent recovery, lying on her stomach for the remaining three weeks. Of course, it'd take longer than three weeks before Scarlet could comfortably sit down again, but I was about to have my abdomen cut open and infinite responsibilities pulled out and legally bound to me.

I was jealous of Scarlet's three final weeks with the plastic butt piece. She was going to play with elephants, hike to waterfalls, and eat foods that neither of us had ever heard of. She would smell and taste and touch things that I maybe hadn't even seen pictures of. She'd see huts in villages, and exotic insects in national parks. The birdwatching would be incredible, not that Scarlet was into birdwatching. That was more of mine and Andy's thing, when we'd go hiking in the state parks. We'd keep lists of the birds and animals that we spotted.

I had been jealous of Scarlet's happy childhood, prosthetic butt notwithstanding. She was pretty. She was an obvious favorite everywhere she went, a child with a halo, doted upon, treated. I wasn't hideous, but I wasn't Scarlet. I had it pretty good, but I'd rather have my anal sphincter chewed from below by a rouge garbage disposal and live with the scarring than have to have gone into the banana room and live with the scarring. She had a light, happy personality; she laughed more than other children. I am scowling in most of my childhood photographs.

Scarlet turned to medical tourism because there are some things that are just this or that side of legal in the United States, and because of insurance technicalities, and because of the embarrassment potential; it was the same sort of reasoning that led her to visit doctors all the way up in Pennsylvania. Wiping was a messy struggle. She had to be so careful not to leave any poop in all of those folds and crevices. Staying clean and smelling fresh were time commitments to which Scarlet was faithful.

It's weird that you spend so much time thinking about your sister's butt, Major Tom said.

It's the fingernails, said the Thin White Duke.

Hmm? I said.

Her fingernails. She bites them. Small, round, cute, but an indication of unresolved stress. The Thin White Duke lounged across his throne. It's the giveaway that all's not well on the inside.

I looked down at my own fingernails. They were long, and painted the red of a fire hydrant. Anne liked to keep them pristine; it imposed a sense of order on the chaos of day to day life. They were always chipped or smeared within minutes of polishing, in the months when Jaimie Taylor graced this world. But they were polished, nevertheless.

She wears a lot of baseball caps, too, Major Tom said, from inside of his astronaut helmet.

My own life hadn't been devoid of solo travel; the summer between high school and my first semester of community college, thanks to my income from the Happiness Hotel, I took the bus up to New York City for five days. I stayed at a youth hostel in Brooklyn. Far from anyone we knew, Elizabeth ran free in parks and on playgrounds, eating many one dollar slices of folded thin crust plain cheese pizza, scampering through some of the largest toy stores in the world, with a budget of three hundred dollars – half from Andy -

for board games, plastic figures, stuffed animals. Free from the judgments of fellow Summers County residents, and responsible for no one but myself, I swung on swings, slid down slides, and even sat in on the edges of a story time with a famous children's book author. It was a magnificent trip. Andy had been so happy for me; he even slipped a card into my suitcase, welcoming whichever cuddly new family members were about to join me on my crowded twin mattress. That's why we dated; because he was the sort of man who could write a card about hitherto-unadopted stuffed animals. And because he shared my longing to have a tail. He knew who I was on the inside, better than Scarlet, my own sister. But still, I was happy for Scarlet, and her baseball caps, going overseas to experience new things, and, in her mind at least, pave the way to happily ever after with some skin grafts and flesh transplants, or whatever it was that she was flying half way around the world to risk infection for.

In order to make Scarlet's three weeks of exploring stretch to look like six weeks to account for her recovery time, I helped her strategize. It was Ziggy Stardust who put it to me that she could wear her black bathing suit bottom, while switching between my three clearance-sale bikini tops (I wear shorts for the bottom), in order to make her beach days look like beach weekends, and so forth. I was the thrift store queen, longing to play dress-up in Amal Clooney's closet, into fashion insofar as fashion can be a point of empowerment. I draped myself in bright colors and adorable animals in order to find kindred spirits. I dipped myself in deep reds and purples, the greens of a thousand forests. I prided myself in knowing which slightly battered straps, beaten buckles, and bruised buttons would draw out bathroom compliments from my fellow females. And I took more than a little satisfaction from the way that Andy eyed me up and down when I twirled before him in nightgowns forgotten since the 1970s, a hole in one armpit, or a bit of lace trim hanging off, but new to me. The budget wasn't as tight back then.

I told Scarlet to pack a plain black t-shirt and a purse stuffed with many different colored scarves in a variety of lightweight fabrics. We went to four thrift stores to pick them out, rummaging through detritus to find swatches of hope to make her pictures from the morning museum and the sunset temple look like they'd happened on different days. Two pairs of sunglasses and one pair of fake clear-lensed glasses as well. Six weeks' worth of photographs in half the time, no sweat. And six weeks as a substitute HR manager, plenty of sweat.

Orange juice.

All throughout school, we played the saxophone. Alto. When we wanted to summon Bowie, we played the Danny Elfman song This Is Halloween, from The Nightmare Before Christmas, only we sang the words in our head differently: This Is Goblin King. I'll play it for you right quick.

Yes, I know, they lyrics are rough. But I was in fifth and sixth grade when I made it up, ok? And back then, it was just the Goblin King and Halloween Jack. Aladdin Sane didn't arrive on the scene until the second week of middle school, once I'd gotten used to my new schedule and gotten on friendly terms with a few kids. I retro-fitted in the other Bowies as they came.

Aladdin Sane went to middle school with us. Our jr. high was a blip somewhere between Jumping Branch Elementary and Hinton

High for just a couple of hundred kids. I knew who ninty-four percent of them were.

My best friend were the Davids Bowie, obviously (I didn't meet Eloise until my freshman year of high school), but I had a few other friends. We weren't a complete loser. Not that all friendless people are losers; in fact, I think they might be on to something. But I sat with two soccer girls and a horse girl at lunch, occasionally reviewed history notes with a quiet boy from my class in the library before the last morning bell rang, rode the bus sitting next to this one girl who chewed gum a lot or this boy who doodled Pokémon on his book covers that were made of brown paper grocery bags, and I got asked for math answers a lot. All of these people made words at me, moved their eyebrows at me, didn't shoo me away. We'd never been popular – bit of a teachers' pet, to be perfectly honest – but the point is, there were only ever like two instances of bullying against me, and nothing dramatic ever came of those.

I was in middle school when Columbine happened. That was the first mass school shooting that I had ever heard of, that practically anyone had ever heard of. You just don't know what it's like unless you have a lot of school memories from the nineties and early two thousands. Today, in 2016, there are multiple mass shootings per week, sometimes per day. But Columbine truly shocked us; some kids walked in and shot some kids. Who does that? Lots of people, nowadays. Shootings are trendy in 2016. All the rage. But back then, Columbine was our JFK assassination.

Scarlet wanted to homeschool the following year. We didn't. I went to a free one month gymnastics trial at a studio downtown. The room was long, and white, and mirrored, and had thick blue gym mats on the floor. Some of the music made me itch, but I liked the class. I had a friend there, Paige, with the blonde braid. She loved kittens, and Power Rangers. The studio also had this springboard thing, like a small uphill diving board, to help you along. It was the same color as the floor in the banana room.

The song Grey Street, by Dave Matthews, had not come out yet, but when I listen to it now, it's what middle school felt like. We were a little forlorn. I talked to my stuffed animals about it. We were worried that we were becoming weirder with age.

Sitting on the edge of the room with the mirrors and the mats and the movements was a boy of ten or eleven, the son of Miss Linda Fay, my gymnastics teacher for the one month in the space of the universe where I am taking gymnastics. Without the observer, is there anything to be observed? What if it's conscious agents all the way down? Not now, Elizabeth. The boy was called Maximino Nicodemo, which he told me was Italian for Greatest Victory Of The People, in Messianic tones.

Miss Linda Fay never saw a gold garment that she didn't want to fondle. She sparkled from her oversized scrunchy to her chipped-but-shimmery soft shoes. There were huge hoop earrings that she took off while talking to us with a huge smile as she stood before the huge mirrors at the beginning of class. A big glittery ring fell sideways on her left hand, because her left hand, like her right hand, was boney. Her nose was also boney; she barely seemed to have a nose. It was like a little skeleton nose. It was as if all of her fat had been sucked out into her hair, which was the color and texture of dead leaves. It was the size of a leaf pile that you could jump into.

There was a bathroom on side three of the studio. It didn't have a bathtub in it, though, so it was a toilet and sink room. I used it to pee one day, at the end of class, and when I opened the door back up, standing there was Maximino Nicodemo, with his slick black hair and his slick black eyes and his slick white smile, looking like a little Mafioso, stumpy as the t-rex on his t-shirt, but puffed up with the confidence of an only child of neurotic narcissists who pour on their child all the praises and defenses that they count like gold for themselves: the child of their loins might as well have been the seventh son of a seventh son, destined to be king. The little twerp rushed up and kissed me on the lips, with his lips, which were spitty. I wiped it off with the back of my hand and Aladdin Sane said, Punch him! I didn't. But I didn't like that this was the world I lived in, the world where people could just ambush you and touch you however they wanted, make you feel fear like some kind of god on an overcast hill, casting lightning.

A feeling like walking through someone's cigarette cloud filled my chest, swirled, plopped into my stomach, slithered through my intestines, and farted its way out of my bottom. I walked over to where Maximino Nicodemo's mom was standing by the stereo, sorting through her cds. This was a long time ago.

I looked up into the moist orbs that she had surrounded with clumpy black mascara, and I said, Miss Linda Fay, what's your last name? And the expired-in-1994 Clifford the Big Red Dog lipstick glooped on her wrinkly anus mouth said, Ferlinghetti.

Butter. Parmesan cheese.

Scarlet had asked me to babysit her black cat, Valentine, while she was away in Thailand getting her butt fixed. Which also meant, while I was filling in at her job and growing a fetus and having a baby and making sure that a baby survived. But yeah, I could change some cat litter. I could hold my breath for long enough. Scarlet Scarborough like the song had a scar on her left wrist, from trying to paint Valentine's claws with bright red nail polish. I liked cats, generally.

I could have done well as a cat. Being fed, and cooed at, and being able to accept or reject pettings as I pleased. Hunting if I wanted, prowling, lounging by day, stalking by night. Valentine had it made.

Elizabeth tugged on my sleeve. At what point does the present become the past? At what point does the future become the present?

I looked down at her mousey brown hair and her wide blue eyes and Anne-me said, Remember what the glowworms say: Grab hands and glow!

We did!

The Happiness Hotel had a big walk-in fridge. I liked to go in there on my break, and stand in the cold darkness, imagining. I'd pretend to be a cave man, or an underwater hyperbaric welder. That was before Jaimie Taylor existed. While Jaimie Taylor existed, I had to nurse, or pump, or feed, or change a baby's diaper on my break.

I stroked Valentine, from the center of her ears to the tip of her sleek black tail. Jaimie Taylor screeched for my attention, or to attract predators to test my defensive skills. It was the middle of the night. I was awake, and petting the cat that I was catsitting, because I couldn't possibly sleep through Jaimie Taylor's desperate screaming, even though I had to be at work in four hours, and had changed her, and fed her, and rocked her, and sung to her. So I gave up. She was going to cry. The inevitable was upon us. What could we do? There was nothing. We stroked the cat. But then the cat rose up and strolled away.

Back when David Bowie existed, ok I know, but you know what I mean, back then, the Council of the Davids Bowie came together to discuss cats. The Thin White Duke thought that being a jungle cat or a house cat was not inherently better than being a human, but wondered whether being a human might entail more than being a cat entailed.

Humans don't even have tails, Major Tom said.

Most of the humans, most of the time, do not have tails, the Thin White Duke conceded, waving his black and white hands, his greyscale hands.

Annieliz Scarborough like the fair looked over at Major Tom. He was a spacesuit. Behind him there was universe material, in shades of green. Major Tom said, Drink some orange juice, Annieliz, or some lemonade. Keep your blood sugar up. Then get some rest. You can lie down, even if you can't sleep. That way, our body gets some rest. We have to go to school tomorrow, with or without sleep.

But without sleep doesn't have to mean without rest, he pleaded to our body, which was pacing up and down. And go use the bathroom, the Thin White Duke interjected. As I did, the Goblin King pontificated: there isn't more to being a human than there is to being a cat, because the experience of being a cat is self-contained and all-encompassing, just like the experience of being a human. If you're a cat, there can't be anything more in the universe than being a cat.

But how do you know that? Aladdin Sane wondered, as he adjusted his seating position on the throne room's lavish Persian rug.

Elizabeth chimed in, How could you know anything about the ontological existentialism of felines?

We had time to do that, to think about things, back when David Bowie existed. The few weeks of quiet between when we stopped going inside of the castle and when Jaimie Taylor came out of our body were not quiet at all. They were fully taken up with the paperwork, the doctors, the funeral, Andy's parents, my parents, starting a new temporary job while keeping up with my old job part time. It was a whirlwind. It was everything Anne could do not to fall apart. Sometimes she did. Sometimes Anne cried.

But then Elizabeth would get scared and get to crying about Frank Ferlinghetti, and bananas, and Nicole's dad, who as lots of girls in my class could tell you, was a kiddie-fiddler. That's not like a violin fiddler or a hey diddle diddle fiddler, either, and sometimes, we're still upset about it. I know it isn't logical; it's over; we get it. But in the past, it's happening, and that freaks us out.

So Anne felt like she shouldn't cry, which was an awful lot like feeling in prison. Eventually, it seemed like her body might as well have just gone to prison, too. Hot meals. Showers. A simple job, parred down to my qualifications. Library books. There'd still be screaming, but not as often. But not as often, right? A mattress.

I thought I'd be a good mother. Since I was already adept at taking care of one little person – me – I thought it'd be a smooth slide of a transition into taking care of one additional little person, who probably wouldn't stay little forever. It had worked out well enough with Martha, but as it happens, a dog is not a baby.

Babies are endless. Sure, they grow up, usually. But there is no break. A dog might be put into a kennel, or out to run through the yard. An infant is infinite. The hunger. The bodily fluids. The screams. The screams.

What have I done? the creature asked itself.

It was way more to handle than I had imagined. There was an overwhelming number of objects. Might as well have been a googolplex. Diapers, nursing bras, cardboard books, pastel animals that rattle when rattled to rattle my brain. Bottles, pacifiers, hunks of plastic in primary colors. The need to learn everything. Not knowing that anything is a thing. Having to be brought to an initial understanding of concepts like temperature and predators, let alone the alphabet, algebra, Al Qaeda. It felt like my brain was trickling out of my ear when I considered the magnitude of everything that Jaimie Taylor would need to learn and have to struggle through. There is a shooting once a week or so in America. Besides, people are mean.

My nipples were bloody. Why, please. The milk that Jaimie Taylor was drinking sometimes was not white or cream, but pink.

Light red. Blood. My blood. Since when were my silk nipples capable of drying out and cracking?

Eventually, it simply didn't happen. Nothing. Not a drop of milk. I had failed as a biological creature. If this had been wild nature, with no formula or bottles, my baby would have either been fostered by another lactating female, or my baby would have died. Most likely died.

Breastfeeding was a black hole consuming all of my time. Bottle feeding was a cycle of nightmares: endless dishes, endless cost of formula after formula toward a line of solid meals ending in liquids and death. They call spouses balls and chains. That's weird. But I can kind of see what they mean, if applied to a baby. She was heavy, like a ball, and was always in proximity to me, like a chain. Chains are heavy, too. At least I made sure that she was well-fed.

Perhaps if Andy had lived, different decisions would have been made. But I had never been so needed. I didn't know what it would feel like. For Jaimie Taylor to exist was for me to be needed. To be Jaimie Taylor was to be in need of me. She had no father. I was it.

I should have thought about that, about what might happen, and how I'd handle it, if my husband suddenly died. He did.

Anger surged through me, red and green and prickly. It filled me with the taste of raw mushrooms and attic dust. I had come to self-awareness in an appalling universe. I was the universe, observing itself, and finding itself, on the whole, unsatisfactory.

I attempted to sit with the sadness. I sat on the floor by the heater, holding Jaimie Taylor the way I used to hold a novel. I felt sorry for her. Her white onesie with the butter yellow flowers accentuated her cuteness. And she was cute, to me at least. An astonishing stretch of time and human development had predisposed me to think so.

I imagined taking her to the Castle Bowie and presenting her to the council. The Davids Bowie cooing over my offspring, whom they would happily help to bring up. But I was alone. No Bowies. No Martha. No Andy, my husband, my boyfriend, my friend, my playmate. I was all by myself, except for Anne.

I'd been especially looking forward to playing with Jaimie Taylor, but so far, I barely had the energy for peek-a-boo. I looked down at Jaimie Taylor. She had begun crying again. She's just expressing herself, I told me, as I glanced at her from various angles, checking the precipitation levels of her diaper. She had just eaten. Perhaps she wasn't finished. But then, she could never be finished, not for the rest of her life. That's how eating works. You consume, and destroy, and defecate, and die.

I felt like I was in that room in Harry Potter, where if you touch things, they multiply, and are hot. That's how it was with all of the baby gear, and that's how it was with all of the feelings. Just stuff, things, out of control, everywhere, chaos, disaster, difficulty.

Nightmares crawled over me and into me as I slept, nightmares of Jaimie Taylor in the clutches of Frank Ferlinghetti. Nightmares of Jaimie Taylor in the banana room. Nightmares of me sacrificing myself, taking her place in the banana room. Nightmares of Elizabeth going through a second round of rounds of torture at the hands of Shaggy the Wizard, among others.

It felt like there was nothing to look forward to. My cute, innocent baby was destined to suffer. Nothing could be worth that. No amount of great life, let alone average West Virginia life, could be worth the accumulated lump of pain, the woundedness of rejection and the attendant panic, of walking through a world where no one had the ability, or inclination, to rescue you from the bottomless pit of the banana room.

Feta.

Before committing to be sexually involved with Andy, the Council of the Davids Bowie put forward that we should go to a therapist and get psychologically evaluated. I was also curious to see if I would test positive for any major psychological disorders. So it was on. I called and set up a time for when the volunteers would be at the Summers County library. One Saturday every other month, the library hosted a program where you could come in and see volunteer therapists for an initial evaluation.

Due to always being the weird kid, I had been tested a couple of times as a child. It always came up the same. Autism, specifically Asperger's, with a few signs of depression. But let's be honest: who doesn't have at least a few of the signs of depression? I used to space out a lot. I'm good at acting normal now; developing the

Davids Bowie helped with that. I internalized more, and acted, like in a movie, almost full time.

Now hear me out. Having autism is not why I killed my baby. This is important. It would be so easy to misunderstand, and blame an action I took on a feature that I have about my brain. Autism is a feature; so is the fact that my eyes are blue. I'm not blue-eyed; I'm Annieliz. I'm not autistic; I'm Annieliz. And Annieliz has blue eyes. Just like Annieliz has autism. See?

And if you're thinking that the perfect logic of those with autism led me to decide to end the life of my child, then you need to ask yourself some questions.

Anyway, the test results pleased me to no end. I still had autism with a side of depression, but nothing else. No schizo-affective disorder, no attention or anxiety disorders, no schizophrenia, no bipolar disorder, no borderline personality disorder, nothing of the sort. And most reassuring of all, no dissociative identity disorder. People with that disorder should not be discounted because of people like me, who might seem similar at first, but do not actually experience life in the that way that they do.

I don't switch between identities – I always present as Annieliz, unified. Only the inside is different. And I don't dissociate - even when I'm at the castle, I'm still aware of my body and surroundings, can still do my work duties, can still carry on conversations with those around me or on the phone; I do not lose time; all of me have all of my memories all of the time; my imagination being vivid is not an illness - and my identities are in good working order. Being more than one person on the inside is not necessarily wrong or disordered in any way. It can be, certainly, but for me, it isn't. Just because the way I am came about largely because of childhood traumas still does not in itself make the way I am inherently negative. I don't keep secrets from ourself – hence sharing this information that you already have full access to at any time. The creature stands in the kitchen, making its list. We are the creature. We like the way we are. Me being we is not a bad thing. But, I knew that already. All of me did. I have mes who are projections, sections, reflections, but all of us are ultimately me. I'm not Humpty Dumpty; I'm David Bowie, and these are the things that I needed to tell myself – it helps to explain it to you this way, so thank you, Mr.

Jones. I feel self-sufficient. Although I still stress-chatter and obsessively narrate to ourself.

We could try those dinosaur-shaped chicken nuggets. No.

One night, late by the cribside, doing our doody duties, a smile crossed my face. I'm not sure where that smile thought it was on its way to.

Andy and I had once tried anal. What a disaster. We got poop on his dick. Because he was Andy, he said, It's only embarrassing if you feel embarrassed. Then we took a shower together.

The next day, I decided to bring Jaimie Taylor into the shower with me, the way I used to do with Martha. She could splash around, I could prevent her from drowning, we'd both get clean, and if she pooped, we'd both get clean again! Jaimie Taylor shrieked the whole time, no matter what temperature or pressure the water was, until the water was turned off.

I didn't start showering until high school. I don't see what the big hurry is, after all. Why not just take baths? In high school, Major Tom and I switched from mostly bathing to mostly showering.

He showed me things in the shower, things that I didn't know we could do before.

I had a few other friends in high school. Like I mentioned, that's where we met Eloise. She looked like she needed someone to reach out to her, so I decided to be the one.

I sat with her at lunch. She reminded me a little of the horsey girl I'd sat with in middle school. We both had sketchbooks. She'd complimented the cover of mine. I'd asked to see the inside of hers.

Inside of mine, I did a different drawing every day. It was like a journal, only I sketched the day, instead of writing about it. And I sketched my day, as opposed to some objective abstract reaching concept of the day, so sometimes there were colorful animals or costumed men or rocket ships and submarines and even trains! And they were parts of my day that you couldn't see, unless you were me, or unless you looked inside my drawings.

I'm afraid that if I stop telling you the truth, then I'll stop knowing what the truth is, the creature said to itself.

I had some friends in high school other than Eloise. There was Nicole, whose dad was a kiddie-fiddler. Four Ashleys were friendly with me, smiled at me, chatted with me in class. The girl whose locker was below mine was called Shelby, and one day, when I opened my locker, my geometry book fell out, and the corner of it hit her right on the top of her head. She made a funny face. Most of the kids kept to their own groups, and didn't bother me, or each other, or as far as I knew, anyone else. Eloise had a lot of friends who wore black fishnets on their arms, and black lipstick on their lips, and black t-shirts on their hearts. So I hung out with them a lot, as well.

One time, Eloise and I were at the house of some of the goths. They had popcorn. They were about to watch some horror movie that we had never heard of. Turned out to be funny; Plan 9 From Outer Space. Eloise and I still reference it to this day. The other kids talked about things, so we talked about things with them, but I mostly only enjoyed Eloise. We drank from our red solo cups, and played our red solo cup games. I wasn't impressed, so I tried acting.

I acted impressed, or innocent, or independent, as it suited my needs. The world is like a computer. You may not fully understand what each piece of every part is doing at the moment, or where it came from, or where it's going to end up when your own carbon has rotten and drifted apart, but you can still change it a little bit, because you are a source of input. You are systems within systems, your gut bacteria like a university, with its own sports teams, within our great big solar system, which is tiny when compared to the local supercluster. So there.

High school was ok. I got made fun of sometimes, and sometimes I still hear those words in my head, but their power has gone out of them, no electricity, no sting, because I think to myself, kids are like that. But then I think, kids become Frank Ferlinghetti.

I put a freshly diapered Jaimie Taylor into her pack-n-play and headed for the toilet, spine tingling, braced for the imminent screams. They came.

I committed a crime. I killed a person. My own daughter. Oh my guts. But that's society's view. And I protected my baby from society. By killing her.

Pancake mix.

Ziggy Stardust also came to me in high school. As shy as
Annieliz and Major Tom were, Ziggy Stardust knew how to blend in
by standing out. His presence revolutionized my wardrobe, and he
asserted himself as chief coordinator of drugstore off-brand
eyeshadows. My hair was artfully dilapidated. Eyebrows and
armpits defiantly natural. Rock on, you hippie chick, Andy had
said, when I mentioned this to him. I wasn't Scarlet, but I would do.
Evan had also been ok with it. Good thing, or else he never would
have been my high school hookup. We kept it legal, and we kept it
wrapped up in both the figurative and literal senses, but from tenth
through twelfth grades, Evan and I were awkward weirdos together.
We made out and more in a variety of spots around the school,
such as the locker rooms and storage closets, and obviously under
the bleachers and on top of teachers' desks, because his father was
one of the two point five (one was a part time guy) janitors, so we
had access to reasonably sneakable keys. Janitors are kind of a
theme with me. After high school, Evan joined the air force.

But before that, we lost our voluntary virginities together, whatever that means. We had sex. Holy hobbits, we liked it! It wasn't quite as fumbly as you might expect of high schoolers. The Tuesday before we'd planned to officially go all the way, Aladdin Sane and Halloween Jack sat me down with a colorfully illustrated book called Jesus Has A Plan For Your Orgasms, and we had ourselves a reading. I was fifteen. So was Evan. We were as prepared as possible, thanks to the simple but direct book from the library at the Castle Bowie: terms like spasm, refractory period, and fifteen to twenty minutes of direct clitoral stimulation, helped to make our undercover adventures chuckleably realistic. Evan frequently gave us Elizabeth's favorite kind of candy, and supplied Anne with calligraphy pens and stationary, though he did not see a difference, nor should he have. Annieliz enjoyed all of his little gifts, even the spooky stuffed octopus. She gave him a leather-bound journal, and a song about dying, and a kiss goodnight.

Evan had large muscles, for a teenager. He was good at the high jump. He took cringe-inducing photos of his biceps in front of the locker room mirror. He slicked his hair sideways and wore a leather jacket, and stood with the posture of a 1950s film star in a black and white poster. He lifted weights. He carried me around like I was some kind of pixie. He made me feel pale pink. Riding on his back like a backpack, or up on his shoulders, or down in his arms. He'd scoop me up, sling me across him, toss me in people's swimming pools when I allowed it. Evan had manners. He could have gone to one of the larger high schools, down where his mom lived. But he didn't.

In addition to the condom coronation, Evan had to, as he put it, get centered. He'd close his eyes, breathe deeply, and tilt his ears down, a couple of times per side. I imagined him pouring various things out of his head through the conduits of his ears when he did this: water, lava, images of other women, aches and pains as colored textures, stress about the future in thought bubbles and slide shows, and sometimes, unfortunately, ear wax. Maybe he was consulting with Bowies of his own.

In high school, I thought about the parasite roulette that was having sex with anyone who could impregnate you. And I thought about it like this: magical powers. Suppose you were given the opportunity to have magical powers: mysterious, seemingly limitless potential, elevated highs of feeling – pride, accomplishment, security, fulfillment, moments of amazing happiness, but at a cost. The cost is at least one death, and at least some suffering. It could be to you. It could be to someone else. It could be to millions of other people. But you won't know. In addition to this gamble and these guarantees, these magical powers are not a gift; you will be billed at sporadic intervals over a period of decades for a sum of no less than but possibly much more than a quarter of a million dollars, and failure to pay this bill could result in death, imprisonment, and loss of the magical powers. So, they're expensive, but they make you feel good. But they're also a lot of hard work to tame and manage – one may become a wizard overnight, but one does not become a capable wizard overnight. But the cost of these good feelings will be collected in more ways than hard work and money, for which you will also have had to work hard. The cost is time. The cost is suffering. The cost is at least one death. And you can acquire the magical powers and all of their attendant costs by accident or victimization by another. Or you can seek them out, go to great lengths bodily and financially to obtain the most precise version of the spell to unleash all other spells. So that's how I thought about children: would I take magical powers under such dubious conditions? No. So, if not even magical powers, then what? Kids? Certainly not yet. Not yet, I told ourself. I should have stopped at, Certainly not.

I had, like Evan, thought that someday, with someone else, I'd have children. We'd both been right. I wondered how it was going for him, if his baby was as much of a crier as Jaimie Taylor, if his wife's vagina, or worse, clitoris, had torn during delivery, if the pounds and stains and grease and arguments that had been added to his life were worthwhile and fulfilling to him. I wondered if he had done the math about how many diapers his child went through in a month. I smiled at Evan when I'd see him at Shoprite, pushing a cart with a baby in a carrier and a toddler making trouble. He smiled back and me, and nodded, the smile filling his face like a pitcher of lemonade, first at the bottom, and then clear up to his hairline. And from a distance of a grocery aisle or a galaxy away, I'd see his smile twinkle its way into a word unspoken: Annieliz, he mouthed at me. The chocolate and marshmallow s'mores of his eyes went as if they'd been through a bonfire as they locked with mine and my lips danced with nary a whisper to say: Evan.

The creature withdrew from such thoughts.

The summer after high school, and all through community college, and after, I worked at the Happiness Hotel. It wasn't really called that by anyone else but me. It reminded me of the hotel of the same name in the movie The Great Muppet Caper. I love that movie! The motel where I worked was shabby but loveable, much like the Happiness Hotel in the film. I did a little bit of everything: front desk shifts, housekeeping shifts, even a bit of maintenance and gardening. I liked it. A little something different every day, changing lightbulbs, folding towels, taking reservations over the phone. The hotel was L-shaped, with white columns. We served a complimentary hot breakfast every morning, and when I worked the late shift, and set up for that morning's breakfast, I got to eat a free meal. That was part of why I kept that job for so long, the pancake machine.

May we please get popsicles? That's a great idea.

When I worked at the Happiness Hotel, I imagined musicals with the Davids Bowie singing in harmony. I wished that I had the skill to write down the notes and whatnot that I was thinking. Perhaps I'll learn. But at the time, I just played these scenarios out in my head, with muppets and Bowies popping up everywhere to sing with me as I did the motel's laundry, keeping the monotony out of the bed-making, and prancing about as I watered the flowers and polished the mirrors. My uniform was black pants and a company shirt, with my hair usually in a messy topknot, but the Davids Bowie wore elaborate costumes everywhere we went. Working at a motel was fun. Thanks to the Goblin King's line about the banana allergy, I was excused from ever doing that part of the breakfast buffet setup.

After the three deaths, I badly missed the Davids Bowie. My shifts at the motel were overhung with drudgery. It might have been a council of Huey, Dewey, and Louie all along. Or Sesame Street characters. It could have been Bernard and Bianca, the cartoon mice from The Rescue Aid Society, but it wasn't. It was David Bowie. It had always been David Bowie. And David Bowie was dead.

The color was sucked out of the work.

I used Jaimie Taylor's baby carrier, with her in it, in her green and yellow onsies, to prop open doors as I did housekeeping. That way, I could keep an eye on her without her being directly in the line of spray of bathroom cleaning chemicals and whanot.

One time some ladies passed by in the hallway where I was cleaning a room. Is this your baby? they said to me from the corridor. Yes, I said from the sudsy tiles of the bathroom floor a few feet away. That's Jaimie Taylor. The two women smiled and one of them said, Isn't he a doll? and I wanted to say, No, she is a person. Then she cried.

When I needed to work at the front desk, I kept Jaimie Taylor in her carrier in the open closet off to the side of where I sat behind the counter, where the computers and telephones were. It was set up so that it could be manned by two people, but only one person was ever scheduled to work the desk on a given shift. My daughter cried, heedless of her location behind a motel desk. My cheeks reddened at the stares of the people I was checking in and out and fetching extra pillows for. They wondered, probably, why I didn't have my baby in daycare, or why I wasn't at home with her, while my husband worked, and what was I, some kind of hussy? Well. Daycare was expensive. My paychecks from the Happiness Hotel kept the electricity and water going at the trailer. That much had to be enough, for right then. I was lucky that Andy and I had gotten married, lucky that he at least had foreseen these possibilities: that one of us might be left alone with Jaimie Taylor and the need of a secure place to raise her. That trailer was the one thing I had going for me.

When it was just me paying for my food, and classes, and stuff for Martha, plus the occasional date or gift for Andy, it was plenty of money. But a baby is surprisingly expensive. Things keep coming up. The need for wipes. How was it that so many got used up? Why did she poop so often? Diaper sizes – how are you supposed to know anything? The words on the packages mean next to nothing. But hey, it could be worse. At least I had a job, and not only that, but a place to stay. And I even had a second job for a while there, to help pay for my hospital expenses. Insurance only covers so much.

Stickers to go on our chore chart!

Jaimie Taylor being born was a boom-boom. Everything is a boom; electrons are booming all the time. Anything that happens. You take out the trash. Boom. But sometimes, big things happen that are lots of little things, too. A terrorist attack. Boom-boom-boom. A tsunami. Boom-boom-boom-boom. But there are things on this scale that go like this: it happens, and it destroys whatever your life once was, and it makes it into something completely new, but nobody else's life is too much affected by it, at least not in immediately perceptible realms. You have a baby. Boom-boom. Turns out, I was only ready for a single boom at a time. Turns out, it was too late. Jaimie Taylor was booming all the time, on full blast. I had meant to turn on a faucet. I hadn't meant to unleash a flood.

The constant physical contact wore me out. She always needed to be held and carried and comforted. This wasn't like with Andy; this was some new person touching me, some other person who I didn't know much of anything about, because frankly, there wasn't much of anything to know. She was blob. She blobbed on. Liquids came out. Of course they did. That's life. Liquids go in. Liquids go out. Solids are the same way. Even gases. Input. Output.

But without Andy here to do it all with me, it wasn't interesting. It was just a bunch of processes. I understood them. Why keep repeating them? To keep the baby alive. So that it could grow up, and have a baby to keep alive. Why, please.

Chili.

There had once been things that enticed me to friendship with Eugene. But it became difficult to conceptualize those. I had thought of him as Indiana Jones, knowing that he could have been an adventurous professor. But he hadn't chosen that. Perhaps I liked my imaginary Eugene better than my external reality Eugene. When he hurt my feelings, some of the group died, leaving others alone. My gladness at seeing him was killed. My comfort in knowing that he was nearby had been undone. Even sadness and anger were corpses; only fear stood strong, with disappointment lingering nearby as a child-sized, emaciated wraith. But obviously, there had once been things.

I didn't understand why he went to the community college. He could have gone to WVU up in Morgantown. He could have gotten an engineering degree, and moved to far-off destinations. But he had chosen life as a fry cook, living in Jumping Branch, West Virginia, a town so small that he had to leave it in order to get to his fry cook job. Why, please.

But then, Andy and I loved and dreamed about this area. The mountains, the leaves. Beauty in death, and all of that. I went to the community college because they had a good two-year hospitality program. I learned about aspects of the hospitality industry, and earned myself a raise at the Happiness Hotel, where my hours of labor counted as an internship and earned me school credit. It was a regular job. I could have done it without the schooling, like Andy had done with his janitorial career. Nevertheless, schooling got me more time with Eloise, and Eugene, and some of Andy's friends. It was a fun experience, going to college. Expensive, but I have cognitive biases justifying it because of the variety of ways in which it spiced up my life. And, as it turns out, working at a motel next to a diner in a microtown is marvelous. If you're into that sort of thing, which we are.

It can be hard to focus on any positive memories of someone when you're afraid of that person, like I had been made afraid of Eugene. But there were a few.

I used to call him you genius, and he crinkled his eyebrows every time, but the crinkles didn't mean the same things every time.

Although I came to associate him with the feeling of I don't want to play this game anymore, we did go to one game where we had quite a nice time. It was a Mountaineers' game, up at WVU in Morgantown. This was before my trust was gone. This was before he'd given Elizabeth one too many scares.

Andy and I were on one of our breaks. Not that we needed to be on a break to hang out with people other than each other. But it was a scheduled part of our relationship. Every six months, our relationship contract would expire, with the option to renew in three weeks' time. It was one of the things that we thought were perfectly normal but turned out not to be, like me asking him how he preferred to be broken up with on our first pseudo-date to Wendy's to not discuss our common nightmares about the banana room, and potentially killing Frank Ferlinghetti.

So I went to the Mountaineers' game with Eugene. I didn't pay that close of attention to the game; hockey is more my thing. I settled in beside him, allowing Elizabeth to roam around the castle, and play with her various friends, including the Davids Bowie. I felt my skin sizzle and pop from the anticipation and occasional brushing touches of my arm or leg with Eugene's. He smiled down at Annieliz with his rabbity teeth and his candlewax face and his flaming eyes. Elizabeth beamed up at him without a plan. That was back when I felt like I could leave my doors unlocked around him.

I wished that I could crawl up in his lap when the moon and the stars came out and lay my head on his shoulder, and wished I could feel him putting his strong and his brave and his protecting around me with his arms. Yep, I wished he'd be there to hold me when I was scared. That was before he made me scared himself.

The creature attempted to grasp its own emotions, and failed ingloriously.

Like I said, I knew that there was some biological detection that Eugene would be a good specimen with whom to mate, but there was more to it than that. He was good with children, and therefore, I thought that perhaps he might be good with me. Obviously I could never call another man Daddy; the concept creeped me out (though I know it's like when people call each other baby). But there were other aspects of the guardian/little relationship, if one wanted to call it that, which were right up my alley. And I supposed that I found him the easiest person to use for certain fantasies: fantasies of me and Jaimie Taylor being taken care of in the aftermath of Andy's death, certainly, but before then, fantasies of me being cuddled and kissed and gently held by someone big, and strong, and committed to not hurting me. I thought about him in this way while on breaks from Andy, and once or thrice while Andy and I were actively together. There were not many men who could accomplish what Andy did, understanding the absurd need to be both wife and child – not his child, not an incest thing, but a child, a vulnerability thing. I could imagine being myself with him. I could imagine him revealing his inner clockwork to me in turn. I could imagine him kissing up and down my body, telling me that he loved every part of me, and both of us knowing the unspoken contexts of the phrase. I could imagine him being, not like Andy, but another loveable incarnation of the proverbial

Man that I was always looking up for. I could imagine him adoring me. I supposed that we adored him; Elizabeth certainly thought a lot of him, before he was scary. At the WVU game, Anne had been tempted to lay a red-manicured hand across the jeans on his left thigh, but we were not at that level of casual understanding with Eugene. I suppose that's where most of the misunderstanding lay: he thought we were on these certain terms, where things like hugs could be dispensed all willy-nilly without proper mutual comprehension of what the definition of a hug is. It exhausted me. We hated to be afraid of him, but fear is not always a choice.

My favorite thing about him was the feeling that if we had been children together, he would have played with me. My second favorite thing about him was that he farted a lot when he was nervous, like at the funeral. I found it cute in its animalishness.

I acknowledge that this is a pinpoint of obsession caused partially, or even mainly, by my need to somehow cope with all of the deaths in my life of late: Andy's, Martha's, David Bowie's, the Davids Bowie's, Jaimie Taylor's, Jaimie Taylor's future's, Jaimie Taylor's possible futures', Andy's future and future life with me, my possible futures with Andy, with that relationship, and as a mother; there was also my own death, potentially, from the brain cyst. So, yeah, sometimes I obsess over little things, rather than think about all of those big things on my plate, a plate which Anne doesn't want to deal with, but which is far too large and heavy and cumbersome for Elizabeth to take on without dropping, and probably breaking, and likely being cut by the pieces of.

The creature held itself at night, a young woman and a younger girl, together in its mind. The creature's breath trembled in reaction to the memories in its brain at night, whether sleeping or trying to sleep, and the creature's spine curled until it was fetal with revulsion. Tears overflowed from the holes in its face.

I was just some girl he knew, a chick he'd had a few classes with. But to me, he was a big star. I admired him for being so complex; a man who spoke the languages of math when he spoke in science and the languages of heaven when he spoke in tongues. He was a Pentecostal, a person given to a certain level of public displays of emotion. It was sweet, watching him, the times when we were in church services together. I liked that he was the type of person who could engage with his inner world so much that he lifted his hands in church. He had a relationship with his God, but he wouldn't talk to me about it. He wasn't embarrassed that it existed, but for some reason – and I suspect that we all know why – he was reticent to talk about the relationship itself, how it worked, other than to say that God spoke to him through impressions and signs – but we are each prone to our own delusions. Andy was Catholic, I'm Methodist, Eugene's an Evangelical. How different are they, really? Pretty different, as a matter of fact, but since when have we been dealing with the facts? Millions of people believe in Santa Claus. We never did; we were not raised to.

Eugene's middle name was Ludwig. His last name was Wrayburn. I didn't mind his homely appearance so much as I minded myself for judging his appearance as homely. But there you have it.

I liked that he was intelligent. I kind of liked that he listened to me for protracted periods of time, but then again, he didn't have much choice, since he was stuck at the fry cook window at Eloise's.

I liked that he was a bit unflappable, like maybe he'd be good in a crisis. His face didn't change much when things caught on fire.

Since his appearance favored Shaggy the Wizard, I supposed that I was attracted to the idea of using a relationship to help me process and overcome my issues. I'm not sure that that has ever turned out well for anyone. In any case, I allowed myself the pleasure of imagining Eugene Ludwig Wrayburn the Good Green Wizard battling and defending me against Shaggy the Evil Red Wizard. For giving me this stage to play on in my mind – for existing – I loved Eugene.

I projected and obsessed and analyzed, but I knew that the fantasies that I'd had of him since Andy's death could never, more than ever, come true, since I put Jaimie Taylor out of her misery.

The creature was lonely.

Pop tarts.

There had always been a second castle, across from the Castle Bowie, far away and out of sight. It was Doubting Castle, from the children's book version of Pilgrim's Progress, by John Bunyan, and

Doubting Castle was occupied by a character from that book, the Giant Despair. His skin was the same greyish blue of what had once been mine and Andy's car. The Davids Bowie and I used to go to this other castle periodically, for me to watch them fight. The six of them would team up with ropes, and skills, and weapons, to take down the giant, time after time, and he'd shake his fist at us from where he lay on the ground, and say, I'll get you next time! as we ran back to the Castle Bowie.

Can we get some Dunkaroos? Pretty please, with sugar on top? As a metaphor, not just on top of the Dunkaroos? We'll see.

We were fit, for a pregnant lady, if I do say so myself. The morning before Andy's funeral, my bruises from the accident still coming into the fullness of purple, we got ourself together, eight and a half months pregnant, and drove over to Cranberry Wilderness for a hike to a waterfall. It was as you'd expect it to be. I was scarlet; I was winded. I sounded like an asthmatic llama. But these things are obvious; it was worth the toil to get to the top and see that water cascading like it was yesterday and like it was tomorrow and like it was right now, onto rocks that had been rocks for millions of years and would be for probably millions more.

I stood there, looking at that might-as-well-be-infinite waterfall, and I spat into it. Andy, Andy, Andy. I pictured flinging my body out into its eternity. Someone would find me, and maybe I'd have split open, and the baby would be out of my belly, splattered and dead. It would be horrible for that person. One or more corpses, waterlogged and probably bloated. Yikes. I hiked back.

I must have looked hideous at the funeral, but for once, I wasn't looking at me. The things that had been Andy were nothing like him now, I assumed. It was a closed casket followed by a cremation. They had strongly advised me not to view any remains. It had perhaps been a mistake to listen, as I had flashes of imaginings of his corpse in various states of decomposition and mutilation, and reality, although maybe worse in its own way, would at least be a singular thing. There were too many realities in my head as it was. These flashes still happen.

Eugene sat beside me. Eloise was on my other side. My parents were behind me. Andy's parents were in the front row of the opposite aisle. As Andy's wife, I got the ashes. I was appalled. We didn't know what to do with them; paint them in a painting, compress the carbon into a diamond and wear him as a ring? The idea of Andy's parents keeping him in a jar on the mantelpiece sent a black-eyed, black-mouthed horror snowman clawing up my spine. I told them that it was my wish to scatter Andy's ashes around the state parks where we had once hiked together. Andy's mother nodded vigorously, tears streaming down her cheeks. His father – the man who had once been Andy's father, but there was no such thing as Andy anymore – put his arm around the woman who had once been Andy's mother. He did not say things. He did not not say them, either.

During the funeral, I desperately wanted Eugene to hold out his hand in an offer for mine, for comfort, but I understood why he didn't. His lips were together, but they were moving. There was tightness about his throat. He farted. He kept farting. He always farted when he got worked up, passionately, like if he wasn't careful, maybe he'd fart out his soul. Eloise sniffed out my need, held out her hand, and held me, that small part of me, the doing bit, at one end of my arm.

I became lost. Lostness was Annieliz. Annieliz was a forest without trails, a country without a name, a planet without a globe. Annieliz's stars had all blinked out. The doors to the Castle Bowie were shut. The drawbridge was up. The lights were off. Everything was dark inside. Everything was dark outside. Everything was dark.

The presiding minister said in dragging, dripping tones that one day we would all be reunited in glory. I sensed the air flickering with unbelief. My body recoiled; this man's own church taught that few are those who find the way. He wasn't saying a funeral for Andy, or for Andy's family. He was saying a funeral. He was generic. He was freeze-dried gospel. He was pollution. This minister wasn't ministering so much as mummifying; we were all going to be united in one thing, death, and what happened afterward wasn't up to us anymore.

I imagined it happening to me. Not the dying part, but being dead. We floated through blackness dotted with stars, and our atoms came apart slowly. We watched it happening to our fingers. Our face had a smile on it. It had happened to Andy already. It would happen to me. It had happened to Martha. It had happened to David Bowie. All the best people were dead. I'd be dead someday, too.

But for the moment, I still had Jaimie Taylor to think of: to usher into life, guide through life, and hopefully not bury.

I was wrong about everything. The only why that I still wondered was, why was I surprised?

I'd wanted to scatter Andy's ashes while Jaimie Taylor was still a newborn, so that she could be strapped to my chest and come along on the hikes. Ha. My abdomen hurt, obviously, but so did other things, and Jaimie Taylor was loud, and fussy, and other hikers didn't need that in their lives. Frankly, we'd have felt rude. It would be unnecessary, not to mention downright uncomfortable for all parties involved, to drag a cranky baby through the cold woods. It was January, after all.

Plus, most of all, having our daughter there would change the experience in ways that I wasn't keen on. I wanted to be able to reflect on my times with Andy without her there. In both senses, without her there. I could maybe bring her along on one short hike toward the end, when she was a few weeks older, to be a part of the scattering, for symbolic emotional purposes. But to be honest, I didn't scatter the ashes until after Jaimie Taylor had had her own funeral and cremation. And yes, I scattered them separately. They were separate people.

Garbage bags.

We lay under soft, warm covers, under soft, warm Christmas lights, nowhere close to Christmas, or right up on it, we lay, naked, breathing. That was all. Me. Andy. All.

It was a good life, the life of a caveman late at night, when another cave man gets up to stir the embers. He was my guardian. We were Snowbear and Littlebear. Sometimes we said or did mean things to each other, but when so, the offended party could say, Goal check! and the other one would have to pause and explain their behavior, the goal that it was trying to accomplish. Sometimes, the other person is trying to be helpful. Sometimes, the other person is trying to be hurtful. It helps everybody involved if there's clarity.

We tried not to say things that would hurt each other's feelings, because we are feelings, and we didn't want to hurt each other. But when we did, we apologized. It was The Andy Standard: apologize every time you scare someone, and every time that you make someone cry, even if it was all unintended. I know that I will never be able to date anyone who does not meet The Andy Standard. So I will probably never date again.

I am the gourmet recipe for going solo: an ex-single-mother, terrified of bananas, child-like, kinky, INFJ, complicated on the inside, with Asperger's, asthma, a brain cyst, a speech impediment, and the proven capacity to be a human killer. In short, unwantable. And still, I obsessed over Wolfgang, and Eugene, in Andy's absence. I was deplorable. A waste of perfectly good universe.

When the baby cries, it'll be like a game, Andy had said. We'll make up imaginary dangers, and then swoop in to rescue her from those scenarios with a bottle or a diaper change. A pacifier is a dragon shield.

That's why I'm in love with you, I said. Then I said, I think we should try breastfeeding. It'll be easier not to lug a breast pump and bottles back and forth to work all the time. I'll have her with me anyway.

Andy said, What's a breast pump?

By the time that Andy had been reduced to a pile of ashes and I'd become someone's mother, I didn't feel much like playing those imaginary games. I tried to. But I felt like a deflated pool toy. Everything was a deflated pool toy.

Ziggy Stardust and I used to have a cave, on the right side of the castle's property. The other Bowies didn't go there. Only me and him. I sat across from him. On his lap, he held Elizabeth. I said, Andy and I are having a baby. It was shortly after I'd told Andy himself, and he'd set me down, from spinning me around the trailer, singing Magic Dance, my feet touching down one second after the final, color-reverberating, Babe.

Ziggy Stardust said, You didn't mean to.

I said, But we'd discussed it, what might happen if I got pregnant. I'm 29, Ziggy. Now's as good a time as any.

Elizabeth turned her head, looking up diagonally into his pale face, with his golden forehead, and his sticking-up hair. But Ziggy Stardust maintained eye contact with Anne across the cave.

I felt like a cave-person, rather than a play-person, in the weeks of Jaimie Taylor's newbornhood. I grunted. Didn't see or speak much to many other people. Felt hot and stuffy or cold and stuffy in the trailer. But it was more than that. My chest was tight. I was lonely, but going out and interacting with people pulled the plug out of my drain and made my internal bathtub empty and gurgley and sad. I kept having the impression that Jaimie Taylor wasn't quite a noun yet. She was still just a verb.

The creature cowered in shame before a longing for its own mother.

Jaimie Taylor never stopped crying for long enough for us to go on a social outing. Every trip to the grocery store, to the post office, to drop off library books that I hadn't had a chance to engage with, ended or began or middled with a gigantic crying squall from my baby. There was no hope of going out to eat, not that I had the spare cash for that anymore, so seeing the crew at Eloise's was out. Going over to someone's house would be a hard sell, too – babysitters routinely charge twenty dollars an hour, and I don't blame them in the slightest. Kids suck. It's not their fault; kids simply haven't had time to become good at being people yet. I was pretty much chained to Jaimie Taylor (and thanks to a gift from Scarlet, I actually did wear her on my chest and back a lot). That was how it would have been in the olden days, though, to a certain extent, so I tried not to think of it as a big deal. It was only temporary, after all. Babies grow up. Usually.

But even an extreme introvert like me needs friends. Without Martha, or Andy, or David Bowie, I was lonely. I saw Frank Ferlinghetti around town, and was afraid that Jaimie Taylor's cries might attract him.

The majority of human interactions I got for weeks on end were stressful ones. Visits to check on Scarlet's butt recovery, employees in my breakroom-office, being barked at by the lady whose dogs we walked on weekends, Dr. Cynthia Hanging, if not by her dogs. My friends did hang out with me, some, coming by the trailer when they could. Eloise made me two cheesecakes. That's friendship. But people are busy, and they have their own lives, and I knew that I couldn't expect them to drop everything and come over when the baby finally achieved naphood. That's not realistic. Plus, more often than not – always, in fact - even half-hour drop-ins were pierced by the screams of my bundle of joy.

I took her to the doctor. The pediatrician was Herbert Spoons. Something is wrong with my baby, I said. I longed to speak with the Thin White Duke about this, and plan out what to say, which questions to ask. I felt lost. I didn't remember when or where I had last slept.

It's just colic, said Dr. Herbert Spoons, his tone enthroned with condescension.

I called my mother. I said, My baby won't stop crying.

She said, You were the same way.

I imagined raising a child like what I had been like as a child. Another incarnation of Annieliz. I vomited.

I was afraid to let my parents to babysit, because that would mean them discovering Jaimie Taylor's intersex condition, and them harassing me about why I hadn't, as they would phrase it, let the doctors fix her. Their religious opinions did not have room for people born with genitals somewhere in between the expected binary.

Aluminum foil.

The day of the sex-revealing sonogram, a blustery, overcast piece of October, Andy and I sat ourselves down on the couch, his arm around me, bowls of ice cream with various toppings mushing together on the coffee table before us. We watched the Hey Arnold! Halloween special. It was ten o'clock in the morning. My appointment was at noon, and I wasn't supposed to eat anything solid until afterward.

Andy drove me to my appointment. I could have driven myself, but on the other hand, driving was uncomfortable, due to the beginnings of a belly that I wasn't used to. So I didn't mind him doing me this favor. Plus, we only had the one car.

The ultrasound technician coughed and left the room. Dr. Wolfgang Savage appeared. His eyes and Andy's eyes touched from a distance. His body swiveled to be more in alignment with my body, and then he said, Well, there's no use putting off the news: the world is going to have a very special baby coming into it, if that's the path you'd like to keep going down.

Andy said, What is that supposed to mean, doc?

Wolfgang Savage glanced at the floor, cleared his throat, and continued, It means that your baby has an intersex condition. The genitals don't fall into a typical male or female category. As to a chromosomal level, we won't know more until –

Andy said, The bleep do you mean, an intersex condition?

We laid our hand on Andy's thigh, and he said, Sorry.

Dr. Savage said, Right, I'm sorry, sir, Annieliz. It's a lot to process. He brought up images on a screen as I was saying, So we don't know whether the baby is going to turn out to be a boy or a girl? Or the baby might have some other gender?

Wolfgang looked at my face. He said, The gender could go in any direction, yes, but that's the case with anyone, really. Most parents opt for surgery while the person is still fresh, but. He didn't say it quite like that. But that's what he meant.

But we'll leave the decision of what to do with their genitals up to them, obviously, I said.

Andy shrugged. It's not like we were going to circumcise, he said. Andy held my hand. The baby's healthy, though? he said. Will it have trouble peeing?

I – I don't think that that will be the case, no, Dr. Savage said, in a smooth brown voice. It wouldn't be what we expect to happen, anyway. I think we should all stay upbeat; there's no need to worry. It's common. About one in every two or three thousand births.

Andy leaned back and exhaled beside me, his hand still around my hand.

Many women choose to abort, Dr. Wolfgang Savage mentioned. But he also said, But if you want a perfectly healthy baby, then you're well on your way to having one.

We went to the car.

We'll pick a gender neutral name, I said, That way, when the child is older, it'll be easier once it lets us know what gender it is.

I've always liked the name Jaimie, Andy said.

It's not as red as Andy, but there's still a lot of red in it, I said, smiling at him with approval.

What's a name you've always liked? Andy asked me. We were driving home. I said, Taylor's got a nice green and gold texture, like springtime.

That is a good one, Andy said, nodding.

Plus there's the red A, I added.

And if she turns out to be a boy, he can go by J.T., if he likes, Andy said.

Yeah, I said, Who are we to get in the way of biology? We are evolutionary experimenters!

The creature shook its head as it remembered.

The good things in life are after me, Anne thought, when Wolfgang Savage breezed through the entryway of my room at the doctor's office. I had an appointment to confirm the pregnancy, as well as get a routine gynecological once-over, since I hadn't had one in ages. Wolfgang Savage was about our age, but we hadn't grown up together. He was doing his residency at Princeton Community Hospital. I'm from Jumping Branch, like Andy, and like Eloise, and like Eugene. But doctor who? Doctor Wolfgang Savage, he was from someplace else, perhaps some other planet. Words like wow were made for Wolfgang. He was awash in sex appeal. His hair swirled. Our temperature rose. If I'd been single, I'd have asked him if he wanted to get coffee, get lunch, get married.

His hands were gentle, and quick to flee, like two baby deer, fawns in the forest, though my vulva was shaved. Hardwood flooring, as Andy and I came to call it.

Wolfgang spoke to me in medium tones. He was an even man, asymmetrical, centered, his speech patterns like plaid tilted sideways. He said, Annieliz, it's intriguing to meet you. It can be a bit awkward for some women to have a young male doctor, so if you'd rather pass on having me do your exam, I understand. Whoever your doctor is, a nurse will be present in the room for the time of the exam.

I relocated my sooty black eyelashes and my frosty blue irises and my not-scarlet-enough-to-be-Scarlet lips and showed him my teeth and told him with words, I don't mind if it's you.

Thank-you notes. Salt and pepper packets from Wendy's, hot sauce packets from Taco Bell; what else do we need to get while we're out?

Between filling in for Scarlet as the human resources lady, my part-time shifts at the Happiness Hotel, and walking Dr. Cynthia Hanging's dogs on Saturday and Sunday afternoons, I had no day off, ever. I walked the dogs with Jaimie Taylor strapped to my chest, because there was no other reasonable option.

There were five of them: Malaria, Chlamydia, Scurvy, Mumps, and Rubella. Malaria was a Pekingese, Chlamydia was a full-sized hunting poodle, Scurvy was a Jack Russell terrier, Mumps was an English bulldog, and Rubella was a French bulldog. Dr. Cynthia Hanging was an orthopedic surgeon, who for reasons that were unclear to him, often made it her business to snoop around Wolfgang Savage's desk area and general person. She was a buxom woman, with thick panty hose, and thicker foundation. Her hair was a suspicious shade of burgundy, and the rotten stumps of what were once teeth festered visibly beneath inadequate dental work. Her partner of unknown gender walked the dogs on weekdays.

On our walks, which by nature were long and arm-straining, to say nothing of spine-shattering, Elizabeth pontificated to Anne as she was carried along. About personhood as a reservoir for joy and sorrow. About the many features of the dinosaur species and their habits and habitats, which she'd devoted so much time to studying. About weight changes since the pregnancy, breast changes since briefly nursing Jaimie Taylor, and how our body hadn't changed this much since Aladdin Sane talked us through our first tampon.

When not doing these paid jobs, it was often necessary to sling Jaimie Taylor onto my back, like the ape that I was, and do the litany of menial chores that no longer came with a singing, dancing Andy.

The creature gathered up sticky pacifiers.

The creature rewashed bottles of indeterminate cleanliness, just in case.

The creature was incredulous, aghast, and flummoxed at the price of formula; twenty dollars a can? It wasn't even the prescription kind!

The creature changed diapers, mooshed up food, and wished for the four thousand, seven hundred, and eighty-third time that month that it owned a dishwasher.

Stores were decorated for Valentine's Day, and then St. Patrick's Day. Easter, all too soon. Minor holidays had not retained their enchantment for me since the three deaths. I wanted to get the excitement back, for Jaimie Taylor's sake, when she was older. I would need to make up family traditions. Special meals. Decorations. But for now, she was a baby, and I was depressed.

The changes in my social structure loomed above me like a skyscraper swaying in the wind. The years of Jaimie Taylor's childhood rushed toward me in a stampede of teachers, doctors, coaches, instructors, and worst of all, other parents. No more drifting around on the edges of society, going to work and coming home and introverting-out. Nope nope nope! Solitude and privacy were things of the past. And here I'd thought my biggest worry would be constantly having to touch and interact with my child. But I had rationalized that, thinking, it's different with Andy; I like touching him. People say it's different when it's your own child, but your own child would still be a sticky, fuzzy, screamy, matted mess, and you should keep that in mind.

Tortillas.

The crib cost one and a half month's grocery budget for two adults. If it hadn't been for Andy's income being one of the hospital janitors, we never could have paid for it. And that was the cheapest crib we could find! I'd have had to make one out of a cardboard box, otherwise. Which sounds good, but I bet it's not long before a baby can get out of a cardboard box with ease.

I had once stood above the empty crib with Andy, smiling down onto its Sesame Street alphabet sheets, which we'd gotten at the thrift store, even though the letters were the wrong colors. Andy put his hand on my belly, and said, I love your tummy, and I love that you're a mummy! We are going to have so many adventures raising this kid, Annieliz. Then we kissed, and he wrapped me up in toilet paper like the other kind of mummy, and called me a mummy mummy, and carried me giggling to our bed, which was really two twin mattresses side by side on the floor with sleeping bags on top to ease the crack. We didn't have a box spring yet.

Once Andy was gone, I only used toilet paper for wiping. My left elbow hurt yellow when I missed him. He brought extra layers of meaning to my life. But then, so did Martha. And David Bowie. I missed having a pug around. It filled my heart with joy to see her stumping about with her curly tail, looking over her shoulder at me with her eyes all wonky, like she'd just been hit upside the head with a frying pan.

Getting to know Martha should have clued me in. Taking care of another living being is not a kinda-sorta commitment. It takes dedication. There are loud noises a lot, and you can't communicate on the same level. Also, the gear, the associated expenses, the time it takes to buy their food and get them fed. Goodness. Traveling with Martha was a handful. Even just a jaunt to the park involved me and Andy harnessing her up with the leash, packing water, usually treats and toys. A baby, though, is an all new nightmare, in terms of clutter. Wrangling the diaper bag and car seat, for instance. You can't leave a newborn behind, not even for a quick trip to the corner store. There could be deaths, arrests, sirens. We hate sirens. They make our neck hurt. Once Jaimie Taylor came about, it was like Martha's puppyhood times ten. Times one hundred. There just kept being more and more stuff everywhere. A fifteen-minute excursion in my old life could easily take one or two hours, with a baby squirming through the mix. She just kept eating, and pooping, like some kind of animal, but I hadn't anticipated having to care for a pet human all by myself. I wished that I could hand her over to Andy for a few minutes. My arms were tired.

So I set her in the overpriced crib, walked into the kitchen, and flung a damp rag around on top of the sticky spots.

Let's pick up something to exfoliate with, one of those sugar scrubs we used to could never afford.

I went through the Liza Fronk room to the glacier, where I played with the penguins and the puffins and the polar bears, while

Anne tried out social media. It was a hassle, having to make a trip all the way to the Summers County Library, just to use the internet. She didn't last long. Especially not after she killed the baby (when I had to go to the glacier from the long way around, through the countryside, without cutting through the castle). Scarlet made a post, and practically everyone we'd ever met sent messages of sympathy and awkwardness. But even before that, Anne hardly ever used social media of any kind. It was icky. It was full of people's presentations of themselves, which were not as interesting as their pretenses to themselves, which is why I'm more of a reddit person; Anne and I spent a lot of time together on reddit, when we did make it over to the library. The other thing that we like to do on the internet is mensa workouts.

The times Anne was on social media, sometimes I peeked over and looked at who had responded to her posts, and proceeded to make up scenarios involving those people for our entertainment. For example, if twenty people liked a photo, five from school, ten from the Happiness Hotel, a neighbor, two friends, Eugene's pastor, and Andy's mom, then I'd visualize all of them together in the jungle, trying to survive, or in cave man days, or dinosaur times, or in a post-collapse future where they were compelled to competitively kill each other. In this way, our friends were like characters.

Having a friend is more than one thing: there's the friendship that each of you make in your minds, based on the friendship that you've mutually put together in external reality, and thirdly, the friendship that you make up with yourself, also in your mind, with a character who looks like, and is based on the idealizations of, that friend.

Social media was so blatantly The Hive. Seeing who posted what, and what they had to say about it, was often depressing. I felt myself becoming more judgmental and sectarian. With reddit, we could simply read the news, and commentary on the news, without having to attach the faces of those with whom we necessarily interacted from day to day. The human race was revolting. The Hive was revolting.

There was one positive thing to be said. Social media helped people take back their middle names. For years, middle names were used almost exclusively for calling a child to a punishment. Middle names were scary. Now, middle names are rising up for endearment, replacing unwanted last names inherited from abusive authority figures, knights galloping for privacy.

I listed myself as Annieliz Scarborough, there, as everywhere, while we were there. It wasn't that I had nothing to hide; we were hiding plenty. But that plenty was locked down tighter than The Truman Show. Big Brother's targeted advertising creeped me out, but apathy is astonishingly muscular. We disappeared, eventually.

Red nail polish. Nail polish remover. Toilet paper.

The castle library had a sunken bathtub. It was perhaps the room I missed the most, apart from the throne room, when David Bowie died. I wished that I could be there, soaking in the steaming tub, eating flakful pastries, bubbles all around me, being read to by Ziggy Stardust, who would be seated at a tea table among the sunny shelves.

But that's not where I was. I was at Jaimie Taylor's funeral.

The preacher was talking about Heaven, but whether or not it existed, and whether or not Jaimie Taylor was there or on her way there, I knew that I would not be going. I had suffocated an innocent life, blown her out like birthday candles. If they knew, I'd be a repugnant monster to their eyes. But all I was, was Annieliz.

Andy's parents took it the worst. I could see it in their eyebrows. My parents could have other grandchildren; still, their tears were thick. But Andy's parents had, I could see, been holding onto some idea of their son in the form of my daughter. I supposed that that was a normal enough reaction, though it made me uncomfortable. His mother's body kept dancing some kind of jitterbug while she sobbed, dabbed at her face with a hanky, and clutched Andy's father's sleeves intermittently. Andy's father's voice was a desert. He said, Annieliz, and he put his hand on my shoulder, and he said, Annieliz, again.

Wolfgang came to the funeral – Herbert Spoons did not - and sat off to one side. I introduced him to Eloise and Eugene, but not as my gynecologist. I just said that he was the doctor who'd delivered Jaimie Taylor. I was glad for those three, and their hugs, and the same was true of my parents, but as for everyone else, they could take a hike. They kept apologizing for the fact that Jaimie

Taylor was gone, having no idea that, at least for thirty seconds or so of my life, that had been the point. Jaimie Taylor wasn't suffering anymore. I was sorry for the pain she'd been through, the pain I'd caused her. But the pain that I'd caused her by killing her was so much less than the pain that I'd caused her by bringing her into this world in the first place, and ultimately, so much less than the pain she would have suffered if she'd continued on in this terrible world. Thanks to me, she wouldn't have to fight her way through the oncoming dystopia riddled with climate change-related plagues, economic collapse, and the artificial intelligence takeover. These people lacked certainty in their own ineptitude. And they kept on touching me: hugs, handshakes, pats between the shoulder blades. I was all touched out, and visibly cringing.

After the service, and the food, and the weeping parents, Eugene drove me and the jar containing Jaimie Taylor's ashes back to the trailer park. I knew that it was not a good idea to drive while in a state of high emotional distress, which is why I'd asked Eugene to do it. That, plus driving the car that I'd bought to replace mine and Andy's car was scary. When I pictured Eugene, I saw a lighthouse on a rocky outcropping of coastline, jutting into the cold salt spray, steadfast in the midst of lashes from waves, from rains, from the cracking whip of lightning. Eugene touched the tip of my nose with his index finger, and I did the same to him. It was our way of hugging when hugging itself would not do. When I exited the car, he did not offer more than silence, but silence was enough.

Paper towels.

Baloo the bear did not respect women. In Talespin, he kept calling Rebekah names that she didn't like, such as Becky and Beckers. But I loved to imagine being Kit Cloudkicker, riding on a board on a string off the back of a plane.

I admired Darkwing Duck for taking in a little girl.

It was not ok that Link insisted on Zelda giving him a kiss before he untied her in that one episode.

Gadget, from Chip and Dale Rescue Rangers, was a role model for me. She always had the right tools, and could fix things in a jiffy. She had male roommates, and a cool job. She was right there in the thick of it, completing missions, not off to the sidelines. I still want to be like Gadget.

Andy had procured many bootleg dvds for me: Gummi Bears, David the Gnome, Grimms' Fairy Tales, Captain N, Gargoyles. He got us a portable dvd player, too, since we didn't have a tv.

Andy was so understanding about my love of cartoons and other things more typically thought of as kid things. He bought me coloring books and things to color with, from time to time. He didn't necessarily participate in, but moreso enabled, my play. Sidewalk chalk and bubble stuff, magic markers, even the occasional costume piece – these were the kinds of things he kept around, and casually gave to me. He also sometimes, God rest his soul, dropped me off at the toy store in Beckley to wander around and play while he did the grocery shopping, knowing how badly going out in public to shop stressed me out.

I would find no other like him; there could be no one else who could give me such a deep level of understanding. The smell of bananas sent me spiraling into vomitous panic; if Andy ever ate them, then he did so beyond my detection. He knew my pain. He knew my secrets. He knew me.

He sang to me when I was fresh out of love songs. I was terrible at singing, not knowing what the desired key was supposed to be, let alone whether or not I was in it. But with the songs that Andy liked to hear, or sing together, that was ok.

It was a bit of our childhood leaking through. We'd be in the car, going along, or doing dishes together, folding laundry, scrubbing stuff. And we'd sing the songs. There's A Hole In The Bucket. There's A Hole In The Bottom Of The Sea. I'm Squishing Up A Baby Bumblebee. Herman The Worm. Guess I'll Go Eat Worms. There Was An Old Lady Who Swallowed A Fly. Found A Peanut. Great Green Gobs Of Greasy Grimy Gopher Guts.

One Saturday, neither of us felt much like hiking, so we marathoned Muppet Babies. We cooked our breakfast together, scrambled eggs with cheese on English muffins, crisp bacon for Andy, a pancake for me. Andy merely smiled when I brought my stuffed Muppets to sit with us on the couch.

Sometimes we built forts! We used pillows, and blankets, and chairs, and couch cushions, and sheets, and Christmas lights. We baked cookies and ate them in there while they were still gooey. Sometimes the cookies were chocolate chip, but sometimes they were sugar cookies with a chocolate kiss nestled on top! Andy took such good care of me. Sometimes he read me bedtime stories, and sometimes, he sat beside me while I read them to myself. Sometimes he'd be propped up on his side of the bed, reading something of his own. Sometimes I read grown-up books, but not always. It depended on whether or not I was sad. If I had a big sad that day, I liked to read a picture book. I can read pretty good for a four-year-old! Well, pretty well. I know all of Anne's words.

Frank Ferlinghetti made us play a game called Genies. A man would polish the gravy boat, and we would have to put our hands on our hips and say, What do you wish for? and then do what he asked. The second wish was usually Charms candy. We and the man both got a piece. The third wish was to hug and set us free. I didn't like the first wish, which was usually for us to lick and suck on a banana. Shaggy the Wizard put his hands over my ears and said, Just like a popsicle, Annieliz.

Sometimes, we had to do a practice popsicle. Frank Ferlinghetti had it, as big as a banana a without a peel, and ugly, but it was the only one we were supposed to use, because everyone else's was dirty. It did not taste like colorful popsicles, either. We would practice with it, and at the end, when all of the practice flavor came out, if we swallowed everything and didn't make a mess, we'd get to have a real, brightly colored popsicle. I never chose yellow.

My favorite bedtime stories?...wow, there are so many to choose from! I like The Monster at the End of This Book, and the Glowworm Glofriends book about the great blanket mix-up. When things are too colorful, or too loud, or the sad is too big, I like to read that book about putting things back where they belong, and with whom they belong. I belong with Andy. But even when I die, I won't be. Good old Andy. Bad, bad Annieliz.

Andy washed the makeup off of my face, gently, one evening after a dinner out. We'd meant to go to a movie, but something or other had upset me. What's important is the kindness that I remember, that kindness of his. His lips were together, but he was smiling. The upper half of his face was still with compassion. He kissed the great big teardrops that were glistening on my cheekbones. The Davids Bowie nodded their approval behind my bewildered eyes.

Aladdin Sane sat facing me, with his legs crossed Indian style. That's what we called it, back then. He held both of my hands in his, and told me to always respect Andy. He said that Andy wanted to be loved for who he was, for existing, rather than for any particular service that he might render.

Keep the end goal in mind, said the Thin White Duke. You want to have a stable relationship, a partner as a reliable source of peace. Do the things that will move toward, rather than away from, the goal of you and Andy both feeling loved, forgiven, accepted. Turn toward Andy. Tell him what's bothering you. The Thin White Duke laid a hand on my left shoulder. Andy can't read your mind, he said. He only knows the things that you tell him with your words, spoken or written. But writing is dangerous; hard to deny feelings sketched out in your own handwriting.

I knew the Thin White Duke to be full of practical advice. He told me that men often experience romance as something that they do for someone else, rather than something that happens to them. But falling in love happens to them, and they want to feel like they're allowed to plummet without working to dig every inch of the shaft they're falling down.

I didn't want romance to be a thing that Andy did for me like he might do a second job – at least, not unless I was his co-worker, sweating on the conveyer belt line. For us, romance was like a pair of pants. We were sewing it together, one pair of pants that had to be adjustable enough to fit both of us. And with neither one of us a trained tailor. We cracked up laughing a lot, trying to make a pair of pants that would fit two people of such divergent shapes. Hence the final push toward the eventual selection of Taylor (tailor) in Jaimie Taylor.

Hair bands – we're down to just one.

If I thought that I could reasonably intervene in a tiger attack to save someone, I would. In the same way, if I saw someone pass out from low potassium, or something like that, I could grab a banana and quickly feed them. But no one would know what an act of sacrifice it had been. I'd rather face the tiger, to be perfectly honest. But what if I'd seen Eloise, or Eugene, or Andy, in need of me touching a banana? That's how much I loved them. That's how much I loved Andy.

He loved me this much: before we had sex for the first time, after a visit with the Council of the Davids Bowie, I determined that, while sneaking under the bleachers with Evan had had its place, I wanted a more traditional, wedding-night-esque experience, and therefore, needed to propose the Peanut Butter Pact (Aladdin Sane's idea), which Andy accepted with alacrity. The Peanut Butter Pact was this: we'd each buy a jar of Peter Pan creamy, and not eat a single thing else for five days. That way, our food budget for that week would be a lot less. And therefore, we'd have money for a night in a motel room. We stayed on the second floor of the Happiness Hotel, which we could afford thanks to my employee discount, combined with having cut back on our normal food intake. I wore new white cotton panties, and a new white cotton sports bra from the plus sized children's section (since I didn't have enough money for adult lingerie).

We had a marvelous time, as expected, and as we were lying in each other's arms after, Ziggy Stardust cleared his throat within my mind. He was holding a picture book called Jesus Has A Plan For Your Intimacy.

I hand-fed Andy with some gummi bears – his favorite – as I explained the proposition, our bodies at peace among twisted sheets.

We should each have hold of a list, was the plan, a list of known fetishes, printed off of the internet. Independently of each other, with absolutely no peeking, we'd go down the list, crossing out whichever ones we were absolutely, under no circumstances willing to try. We'd leave blank the ones that didn't sound appealing or unappealing. Stars by whichever ones we knew we were individually interested in. And then, we'd work our way down the list, trying different things, maybe a new fetish each week, to discover what else we liked, and what all that we might have in common.

There were more than four hundred common kinks, and at the time of Andy's death, we'd found twelve that we could both enjoy. Sex doesn't always need to be romantic; sometimes it's just funny. Sex with Andy was downright hilarious. He taught me the value of wackiness, of laughter as relief. It wasn't so much the kinks themselves as it was us building up a host of memories between just us two: memories of tenderness, animal noises, hysterical laughter, and sometimes, abrupt, panicked crying. It was the full intimacy package. He could say what was on his mind, what was on his heart. And I was on his heart, my ear to his chest, his arms enfolding me, his embrace consuming me.

Spaghetti.

If my calculations are correct, then Jaimie Taylor was conceived on a Saturday, in the Cranberry Wilderness. There were cracks in reality, then, but not as many. We walked at my pace, slightly slower than Andy's natural pace, as his legs were considerably longer, and Andy said, I love how we can just be, and don't have to talk. And I said, Yep.

The thing about going to the grocery store is, seeing other people near bananas. I can dodge the banana display myself, giving it a wide berth, but they don't know. And seeing, say, a woman pushing a cart with bananas in it, gives me the same feeling as if the woman were carting around a venomous viper.

The creature allowed itself the pleasure of ruminating on the fact that at least no one else knew these thoughts.

Not another creature alive on this planet knew, now that Andy wasn't on this planet anymore. Andy wasn't anywhere. Andy wasn't Andy anymore.

The path was crumbly and the path was brown. I didn't know what I was getting into. I was more realistic than Andy about the idea of growing our family; he had a case of Kodakitis. Andy, my beautiful boyfriend, waltzed down the path toward the waterfall, waltzed down the path toward parenthood, waltzed down the path he'd been set on since the moment of the Big Bang. He was picturing games of catch behind the trailer with his eight or nine year-old-son. He was thinking of diapers in terms of some detached, existential experience that he'd go through a couple of times. But we knew. Our mother had told us. Scarlet sometimes went through up to twelve diapers a day. Twelve. I had seen children. It's different, if you've just been one. But I'd volunteered Sunday and Wednesday nights in the nursery at Eugene's church a few times. And there were often kids as guests at the Happiness Hotel, kids whose parents had left their parenting skills at home. Why did a motel even need to exist in a place as small as Beckley, West Virginia? But there we were. Eugene, at Chez Eloise or at the Pentecostal church, and me, also working in Beckley. The motel being next to the diner was convenient. It was worth the money I paid for breakfast every day (fifty percent off, the best friend discount) to spend that much more time with Eloise and, let's be honest, Eugene. It wasn't a crush. It was an obsession without being an infatuation. I wanted him. That was all. But not until after Andy died; before just wasn't like after at all. All of that to say: when it came to prospective parenthood, Andy had on his rose-colored glasses. I didn't blame him. He'd been spoon-fed society's story of fatherhood. It'd be leather gifts on Father's Day for him, but

I knew that it would be a lot of adjustments and hard work. I was ready for adjustments and hard work, mind; we all were, even Andy, though he wasn't quite as prepared as the rest of us. Still, I hadn't thought it out like I should have. Hindsight.

So there we were: hiking to hook up. It wasn't particularly unusual for us; making out and having sex outside were good old-fashioned fun. We weren't actively planning to whip up a fetus, but were down to condoms only, since hormonal birth control was unacceptable to my body, and I couldn't face anyone – gynecologist or no – inserting an IUD at that point in my mental health journey, plus we were on the verge of getting old for first time parents, by southern West Virginia standards, and we were, with two incomes, more or less financially prepared. Except that you can't be prepared for something like having children; it's the ultimate gamble.

Andy took off his jeans and cast them into the bushes, out of sight. He stood in his boxers, understanding me perfectly. It went unspoken, but he could tolerate jeans, and I could not, due to the way that jeans had been used against us in the banana room. I had never had to explain it to Andy; he knew, because he'd been there. It was ok that I didn't know how to explain.

We were off of the trail, had gone through the woods into a meadow. There were purple flowers, and there were yellow flowers, and there were prickly green weeds. We had brought a sleeping bag. Andy unzipped it.

I unzipped my vest. I stepped out of my capri leggings. They were grey, Andy's third favorite color. He cupped my breasts in his hands.

The creature paused in the writing of its grocery list, and brought a fingertip to its mouth, recalling.

I was in the breakroom. The breakroom in the gynecology wing of the Princeton Community Hospital was a third of the size of my trailer, and every wall was lined with counters, cupboards, and shelves. There was a watercooler. My desk was the table in the middle of the room where people sat to eat lunch. Scarlet's computer looked bare and out of place at the otherwise vacant white table. A deep pool of gladness sat at the bottom of my heart, and into it poured a waterfall, and that waterfall was falling from the fact that Scarlet's actual office was being renovated. It wasn't just the job; income itself was important to save up for Jaimie Taylor's arrival, but with Andy not being an entity anymore, I was relieved to have the distraction of Wolfgang Savage prowling through, taking his breaks, eating his lunches.

He approached the refrigerator. Got out a brown paper bag with his name written in tiny letters in the upper right hand corner. He sat perpendicular to me, so that I was at his right hand. I liked being where I was. I liked him being there. I had long dreamed Andy into this position, even after he was there. But he wasn't there anymore. So I was happy to have Dr. Savage sitting at the head of my table.

He said, Annieliz, I want to know you.

I pulled up the reins on my heartbeat, and it slowed to a standstill.

We've been working together, well, kind of, for weeks now, he continued. You're doing a great job as the fill-in. But tell me about you. Scarlet never did say very much.

I wanted to tell him that having David Bowie in my head had been like having my own personal Spice Girls, but that my dream team had been crushed, cursed, destroyed, demolished, wiped out, put to death, and laid to waste, by Bowie's cancer. The real Bowie's cancer. He had died. Martha had died. Andy had died. I was left where I was, right where I was, alone.

Instead, I spoke these words to Wolfgang Savage: It's been a big month. I can't believe I'm about to be a mom.

And then, to my utter flabbergastation, Wolfgang extended his arm, and briefly curled his fingers around my palm. He gave a mild squeeze. I know, he said. He withdrew his hand, got out his sandwich, and unwrapped it. After swallowing the first big bite, he said, Let me know if there's any way that I can help you out, be there for you. I mean that. He tore off the corner of his lunch bag that had his name written on it, and asked me for a pen. I handed him mine.

I want you to have my cell phone number, he said, to call if there's an emergency. If you go into labor early, or something. I'm sorry if this is inappropriate. But since you've just lost your husband, I don't want to be condescending, I just, the thing is.

Thank you, I said. Make love to me on this table, I thought.

It was not apparent why he wanted me to call him personally, rather than just come to the hospital, if I went into labor. We had scheduled a c-section, but it could obviously be moved, and done by whichever doctor happened to be on duty. I accepted his number when he handed me the torn off corner of his bag, though.

I rolled it up like a tiny brown scroll, tucked it between my tits, and said, When you paint, you have to keep dipping the paintbrush in to get more and more paint on it. But then, when you try to rinse it, cascades of paint just keep on coming out. Like its been hoarding colors inside of itself, trying to make a personality.

He stared at my face in much the same way that he'd stared at my vagina the first time he'd seen it, surveying the damage from the banana room. The scarring was on the inside. He stared at the scars with his fingers, hmm-ing quietly. And now he stared at my face, as if I were a paintbrush, hoarding colors, which he was trying to rinse.

Do you paint much, Annieliz? he said. He was eating Fig Newtons. I hadn't had a Fig Newton since fifth grade. Halloween Jack and I had eaten them on the playground, having snuck them out after lunch, having not had the appetite to finish them at lunch. We sat by ourself in a shadowy patch of pavement. It was the Monday after we'd spent Saturday night at Nicole's house, for her birthday. We had pepperoni pizza that night. I haven't eaten a pepperoni since then, either. Not on purpose. Never noticed 'til now, not about the Fig Newtons, either.

I said to Wolfgang Savage, over the top of Scarlet's white computer, Yeah, I paint sometimes. I mostly draw, though.

He smiled at me, kindness crinkling the skin around his beef stew eyes. Landscapes? he ventured.

I looked down at the surface of the table in front of Scarlet's keyboard. Yeah, I said, Animals, landscapes, outer space. Whatever. I waved my hand a little. I felt how well he could see my stupidity.

He crumpled up his paper bag and stood up, moving toward the trash can. He said, Show me sometime.

The creature was a blundering fool.

They had asked me not to eat or drink anything for eight hours prior to my C-section. Already, misery. Irritation. And the baby wasn't even here yet.

My anxiety was raging, peeking, trembling, and rationality was feeling limited, but it was there. When Wolfgang Savage, M.D., peeped his head around the door and asked if I was sure, we said Yes. He asked this not mostly because of the C-section itself, but because I had elected to have both of my fallopian tubes removed as well, to prevent further biological children. He went away, and the person with the drugs came, and added things to my IV drip. It was abdominal surgery, but at least my vagina wouldn't tear, and my butthole wouldn't tear, and most importantly of all, my clitoris wouldn't tear. That's a thing. That can happen. That does happen to a lot of women. And one mustn't forget, one's clitoris is forever.

It wasn't the sort of thing that makes a body unconscious, but rather just enough to make one loopy and out of sorts, to not respond to pain in the usual ways. I could feel tingles in my thighs, shoulders, hips, and butt cheeks. My muscles progressively relaxed all over, and my mind felt untethered. I knew that it was because of the IV drip, and that much doom awaited me. But I floated along with it, knowing that at this point, some things were inevitable.

As I felt my body melting into the chair, they wheeled me away. I was helped onto some sort of gurney, or perhaps surgical table, and Dr. Savage reappeared.

Begowned, and my feet bestirrupped, Wolfgang stuck his torso between my knees. I considered freaking out, but drugs being what they are, I remained still and outwardly placid. I realized that he was putting in a catheter or equivalent torture device; it hurt, but I was able to disregard the hurting pretty thoroughly. A ball of nervous tingles gathered together in my stomach, crackling with anxious light, and worked its way up into my throat. I dry-heaved, twice. Elizabeth was concerned.

The creature did not know what to make of itself.

I tuned my drug-addled brain to a channel where Wolfgang Savage was between my legs for another purpose. This fantasy, chemically aided into hallucination, took over, as if I were the audience, and not the director. The nurses vanished. Dr. Savage morphed into a dream, and in its beginning, Wolfgang lapped at my vulva like a cat. Another part of my brain wondered if my body would go into orgasms on the delivery table. We collectively decided not to, but to continue with the fantasy reel anyhow. We could watch it later. The dream of Wolfgang drew up close to my face, and kissed me with the wetness of my vagina fresh on his lips. His tongue colluded with mine, conspired with mine, collected and clevered and collapsed with mine. Our tongues were in synchronicity, complementing each other without hesitation or misstep, each movement perfectly unified, like two tentacles of the same octopus.

Shivers ran through my body, each vertebra quivering in a different color. Pain sliced across our belly with the heat and breathtaking force of a volcano. My thighs and pelvis clenched like a vice. Wolfgang's hands were present in my abdomen, moving like a second and third animal on either side of my fetus. The dream of Wolfgang presented me with my daughter, kissed me on the cheek, and declared his wish to adopt her and marry me. A quick version of our lives spun out within me, up until dying as roommates in a nursing home run by robots. The real Wolfgang gently moved aside the top of my gown, as planned, and laid a slimy glowworm, stitched together with screeches, upon my chest. She was ok.

She's come out just like we expected, Dr. Wolfgang Savage said, softly, and with a soft smile. He meant the intersex condition. It was a big deal, to medical types, even though they must have learned in medical school how common these things are. I shrugged as best one can shrug with a baby one one's shoulder and a hole in one's torso. Other people were stitching me up or taking out my fallopian tubes or removing my placenta or contracting my uterus or whatever; I, drugs still in full swing, was now awash in weird post-birth hormones, and wondering if I was going to burst into sobs in front of Dr. Savage.

At least I'd saved myself the near-inevitability of pooping in front of him, had I gone the traditional route. Women poop on the table. It's part of pushing out the baby. Hence, one more reason to not push. Or to never have a kid in the first place. Like why would you? Really.

Of course, much as I fixated on him, I did have bigger fish to fry than humiliating myself in front of the hot delivery doctor. As if he could ever see a crime scene such as my innards and proceed to find me outwardly attractive. I almost dreaded looking at the baby. My baby. Oh my guts.

Relief at not being pregnant anymore seeped in. But so seeped reality: I was no longer a free woman. I had just entered in to the ultimate relationship: creator and creation. I could raise a great person. But I could have been a great person myself, and I wasn't. I was average. She would probably be average. Most people were. Or she might have turned out to be a human killer, if I hadn't turned out to be exactly that myself. Like mother like daughter.

For three days, I snuggled the glowworm in the black hole of the hospital bed, with Dr. Savage popping in occasionally, my husband never, David Bowie never. It was supposed to be over, but everything hurt. My butthole hurt. Why, please.

Eventually, it was all said and done. The papers were signed. The shots were shot. Eloise and my mother were waiting in the hallway. My father was in the lobby. My parents drove me back to the trailer, with Eloise following. Eloise held open the door, and my parents saw me and Jaimie Taylor inside. They left, with kisses left upon cheeks. Eloise stayed, with a furrowed brow. There was a lot of blood. She didn't care for children. But she cared for me.

Do you realize, we don't have to do the Wendy's run for salt and pepper packets, or go to Taco Bell for hot sauce? We can buy that stuff. But don't you see? We need to keep watching our budget. We're only grocery splurging for this one month before we leave. We should still cut corners, though. You never know what might happen.

I found it bizarrely alluring that a man as bright as Eugene went and got himself mixed up in something like Pentecostal Evangelical Christianity, one of the weirder branches. In the days when Jaimie Taylor existed, I went to his church often, for the free childcare. That's right: in the same church where I once worked the nursery, I now dropped my kid off in the nursery, and sat through services, to get a break. It was like Jesus Camp every Sunday.

Do I believe in God? Well, that depends on what you mean by God. There was a mighty big number – I didn't know that number's name, but I knew that it would be there if it was looked for it in the right way, called upon correctly – and that was the number of things that people sometimes meant when they sometimes said the word God. I prefer to contemplate the many things that people might mean, and keep my own meanings to myself, Mr. Jones, so feel free to look around.

Annieliz stood in the sanctuary of Calvary Assembly of God, singing along, watching the other apes raise their hands, listening to the other apes speak in tongues. That was ok. That was their thing. But their ok thing was weird, and so were the other ape creatures. Ape creatures always were.

The long-bodied being who resembled Jake, the yellow dog with glasses from Adventure Time, called Eugene, spent a lot of his life volunteering for the church. His beard sat curled around his chin, like an animal guardian poised to drip wisdom in languid tones, his moustache its tail.

Eloise was not a Pentecostal herself, but she also often attended Eugene's church, for anthropological reasons. She moved, in her opinion, like an awkward giraffe, tall, tall, tall. But I often saw her as a graceful being, like the hippopotamus ballet dancers from Fantasia. Not ballerinas; the ballerina is the special one in the middle.

I wondered if anyone in the church could be the reddit cumbox guy. They didn't need to be the actual guy; just to be equivalently human. That guy – oh, he was this guy who, like how guys come in a sock, but he'd come in this shoe box, a cardboard shoebox, all crusty, and he kept it for a long time, and we saw pictures of its evolution on the internet. That was a secret that he kept, under his bed or somewhere.

Frank Ferlinghetti's mouth was a cemetery: neat, well-kept, clean, and dead. The smell that surrounded his whitewashed gravestone teeth was the smell of toothpaste and orange juice. He always talked silly in front of us children, even when speaking to adults. Once he told Shaggy the Wizard, Quit tooting your jizz trumpet and frost this little cupcake. Shaggy the Wizard sometimes took off the banana peel and used the inside as a magic wand. He could squirt sore throat medicine out of it and I would crawl around and lick it up just like they told me to so that I wouldn't get frogs in my mouth.

The preacher started talking about that time when Jesus met a man who tended to wander around naked among tombs. Jesus asks the man, What is your name? And the man replies, My name is Legion, for we are many.

I was always relating to the wrong people in Bible stories. It's the potential for misunderstandings based on passages like this that keeps me from telling the secret of what I'm like on the inside to anyone, including those closest to me. Psychological evaluation in hand or not, they would deem me insane. But we aren't.

I might have gone to Eugene's church, even without Jaimie Taylor, without needing the nursery to hold her for a while. The nursery workers knew about Jaimie Taylor's intersex condition; I spoke to them about it when I signed her up, since they'd be changing some diapers. They blanched, wide-eyed at my description, the prettiest girl's mouth going into a wide frownish thing, like a platypus's bill. I explained briefly about wanting to keep this private, at which words they nodded vigorously, unblinkingly. I sighed about it. But I liked Eugene's church, overall. Sometimes it was scary, but Elizabeth liked testing herself in scary situations.

There was always a crowd, and it was loud, and people were huggy. They wanted to shake hands. They wanted to make small talk. The colors and sounds and touches were too much on my autism and my synesthesia, and my speech impediment made nearly all social interactions a nightmare. So, perhaps I wouldn't have chosen to go there on my own after all. I hardly ever had, in the time between when I volunteered in the church nursery, and when I put my baby in the church nursery for a wee bit of relief.

There was an altar call. I glanced at the sound booth; Eugene was in his usual spot. It was a perfect excuse for him to never have to go up front. Going up there was terrifying stuff. The people wanted to lay hands on us, and shout stuff at us, and if they knew the way we are inside, they'd do even scarier stuff, in order to try and cast out demons. But there aren't any demons. It's only me.

I slipped out of the main service in the sanctuary and headed for the bathroom to wait out my maximum childcare time. I could still hear the music.

Liquid soap, refill of inhaler prescription, gummi vitamins.

Halloween Jack could turn into a giant bird, and back then, sometimes we flew around on him - on his back, or in his claws. The bird was different colors every time. Sometimes I put the bird Halloween Jacks on Andy's birthday and half-birthday and unbirthday cakes. I suppose that he attributed them to our shared love of birdwatching in state parks.

Last year, we were tent camping in my dinosaur tent in the back yard patch behind the trailer, and I brought out Andy's cake. On it, there was a red dragon, and the red dragon was playing the saxophone. Andy asked about him. His name was Norbert. Andy asked if he was named after the dragon Norbert in Harry Potter, but he wasn't. He was a character in a book by Halloween Jack, called Better Ask, Norbert!, which is about a dragon who wants to take a princess back to his cave-castle, tie her up, and play his saxophone for her. But it's important to always ask for people's permission.

That's the lesson of the book. Norbert asks the princess if she wants

to be taken to his lair, and if she wants to be tied up, and if she

wants to experience his saxophone and its colorful performance.

Halloween Jack read it to me, in fourth grade. I drew out all of the

pictures, too, in one of my old sketch journals. I showed them to

Andy, and he looked at them with his lips apart.

That led me to share some more Bowie-based art with him,

this time some recent sketches based on a book that the Goblin

King had read to me back in first grade, in the cemetery in the

shadow of the volcano beyond the jungle beyond the forest behind

the castle. It was called It's Ok To Say No, and it was about a family

of kangaroos. The mommy and daddy kangaroo learned that they

shouldn't make their joeys hug relatives on holidays, or school

bullies when making up, or stay with someone whom they find

objectionable. And the joeys learned that it's ok to say no to anyone

who tries to touch you in ways that you don't feel ok with, even if

that person is a doctor, or a parent. And if they don't listen to no,

it's time to find new grown-ups.

Andy and I had been going out regularly for a while by the time he found out about the imaginary books. He seemed to hold my hand more often after.

A block of pepper jack cheese. Since you said we're splurging.

When we inherited the trailer from Andy's grandmother, we also inherited her claw-footed bathtub, which by this time might be worth almost as much as the trailer itself. I had looked them up online at the library; a new one cost at least as much as a year's utility bills.

Martha's body had been in the back seat of the car when we were hit, in a white cardboard coffin. In the chaos, the towing company or someone got rid of those things which had once been Martha, as I had known would probably happen. She didn't get a proper grave.

I thought it over as I sank into the bathtub one day, Jaimie Taylor strapped into a wee rocking swing on the bulging and buckling wood of the bathroom floor. I had tried to do right by Martha, putting up a little memorial stone in the back garden. I could almost touch the other trailers from the porch affixed to the back of mine.

I wondered where I'd be without the enormous privilege of marrying Andy and inheriting the trailer.

Jaimie Taylor shrieked. I glanced over from within the bathtub. She had just been fed and changed. I sang to her. I sang what Andy and I had planned to be her special lullaby, the song Marvelous Things, by Eisley. She continued to shriek.

The creature projected a series of possible reasons as to why its offspring might be wailing with such persistent vigor. Perhaps a poisonous gas detectable only to infants had leaked into the room. Perhaps a predator was just beyond the walls. Perhaps she had been given a vision of the future, and had seen Frank Ferlinghetti in it.

Breathing in, I heaved myself out of the water, and picked up the rocker seat, with Jaimie Taylor still strapped in it. I padded down the short hall, naked and dripping, and left the source of the screams at the other end of the trailer.

I lowered myself back into the water. It was still a little better than lukewarm. I got back out before twenty seconds had passed. The neighbors would come knocking, and when they did, I couldn't be on the other side of the residence from my baby, not even trying to comfort her. You could hear water boiling in the trailer next door. You could hear a cat stretching in the trailer on my other side. You'd be able to hear Jaimie Taylor for miles around, attracting zombies, puncturing eardrums. I pictured her as a shock rocker, grown up and on stage, screaming these same screams, but as lyrics, black makeup smudging in the sweat of performance adrenaline.

I put on what had once been a fuzzy red bathrobe, now faded and thin, also an inheritance from Andy's grandmother, unstrapped Jaimie Taylor, and bounced her on my hip. I sang Jaimie Taylor another song, a song of Andy's. I closed my eyes. Andy, Andy.

I don't know why she swallowed the fly.

Back when Andy existed, I'd take a bath almost every day. Often but not always a bubble bath. Andy treated me with colorful foams that you could sculpt, and a pillow that suctioned on to the tub, and never a word of criticism about the fact that I still had and used my rubber duck from childhood. And other bath toys. He just knew. Well, also, we discussed it, like the adults who we were. He even got me a rubber duck that vibrated, and he bathed me, since he was the perfect man. Also because we communicated our preferences like rational beings. I didn't expect him to do all of that, but he said from the beginning that his janitor income was being wasted on cigarettes and could be better spent anyway. Never on stuffed animals, though; it makes us nervous just thinking about it. You can't introduce a new personality into the family all willy-nilly like that. The rubber duck had been mutually agreed upon beforehand.

I spent a lot of time at the Castle Bowie when I was in the bathtub. When I sank in, and put my head under water, it was to listen, or to pretend fates, or blow bubbles, or even scream, to see what it sounded like. But the day came when I dipped my head under the bathwater to scream for other reasons.

Sometimes I left Elizabeth to splash around the tub while Anne went to the castle to discuss matters of import with the

Council of the Davids Bowie, anything from what to get at the grocery store in order to prepare dinner later to which fetishes to test out with Andy to listing out things that Andy and I would need to do in preparation for expanding our family. My problems were different then; it was easy enough for the Thin White Duke to hammer out a budget or select a birthday gift for Scarlet. I wondered how he'd do when faced with the particulars of the intersex condition that the ultrasound had revealed, or how he'd fair once the vacation plans had a stroller and a diaper bag and a pack-n-play added to the logistics. I wondered about all of the wacky things that Ziggy Stardust would come up with to entertain the baby. I never thought they wouldn't be here. I never thought they wouldn't be.

One time, shortly before Andy and I had gotten reacquainted, I'd been in the bathtub, chatting with Major Tom, having myself a warm, quiet think. And I said, if I ever get married, I want it to be to a man who feels like an old pair of slippers, like Eugene. And Major Tom said, Eugene is like Eugene.

But then, Andy.

Andy, who swapped full body naked massages with me. Andy, who slept in with me on the weekends, took me hiking in state parks, and helped me make a pancake dinner afterward. Sometimes, the pancakes were shaped like Mickey Mouse. Andy was an artist.

It had been the plan for Andy to take on most of the cooking, while I did most of the cleaning, just like it was in our lives already. When Jaimie Taylor arrived, and all throughout her growing up, she would know the love of her father from his labors over stove and counter, plate and pot. He'd make all of her favorite dishes, which were sure to be different from our favorite dishes, because she'd be her own unique person. And Andy would nourish her, and indulge her, and feed her, as he did to me, and our gladness would be multiplied.

When she was older, I supposed I'd set up a sticker chart or other reward system for passing off my least favorite chores, like dishes. And I'd teach her how to do laundry, as my mother never taught me. She was a good mother. But it didn't necessarily occur to her that one day I'd be living on my own.

There's a hole in the bucket, dear Liza, dear Liza.

It's just the two of me. I'm the only one in here.

The creature was alone.

Body upon bed, I went over unrealistic scenarios. A guy repairing my non-existent laptop being stumped and turning to Eugene for help (at least I imagined him as intelligent), and Eugene therefore seeing the highs and lows of my internet history, not to mention the stuff I wrote about him in the journal folder on my desktop, which I would have definitely written my secrets in, if I'd had a computer. But then, as I kept thinking about it, I thought, would anything really shock Eugene? Probably not. I'd spent many a Saturday morning lingering on the cherry barstool, oversharing every manner of embarrassing childhood behavior, work mishaps, everything short of specific sexual proclivities. So what if he read my internet search history and saw what kind of porn I was into? Or would have been, if I wasn't always at the library when I used the internet. Who cares if he judges us? We're not doing much better or worse than anyone in our equivalent situation, minus the bit about killing the baby, which I suppose cannot, after all, be a matter of a minus.

Bagels.

Elizabeth used to smile up at Andy and say, Guess who loves you? And Andy would say, Who? And I'd say, I do! And I did. And he loved me back. The one who loved me back is dead.

Cream cheese.

Long ago, Ziggy Stardust told another story.

There was a man stuck on a roller coaster at the end of the world. He had been the only one riding when mankind came to an end. And now he was stuck riding it, over and over, unable to escape.

The man could not know that the world had ended; he might assume that some local disaster was delaying his rescue, but it might be hours before he lost hope.

Perhaps his organs were rupturing, or he had lost consciousness, from being on the ride so long, all of that speed, all of those loops, the twists twisting him. For days.

Photographs of his face in various stages of screaming and shocked silence were played back before him as he whizzed past a giant screen near what should have been the end of the coaster. But he had no way to unstrap himself. And no way to die, except from thirst.

The roller coaster was pale green. The man's skin became pale green, and stopped being skin.

It was unlikely, but that did not preclude it from being one of the possible fates that might befall a person.

Ranch.

When I got to feeling overwhelmed, I unfortunately tended to do what my parents called lawyering. They, and Eugene, actually, have said that I sound like a prosecuting attorney. And I suppose they're right. Here's why.

Anne appeared to have a waitress or cheerleader personality, but was, all in all, still an introvert. She could sometimes manage to be charming. It had happened once or thrice. But when Anne was too overwhelmed with bright lights and colors and noises and humans pressing in, and sensory overload came about, or the stresses of the day or of the lifetime were too much to bear, or the invasive splashes of memory when Frank Ferlinghetti and Shaggy the Wizard and others here and there drag me back through my mind to the banana room and its attendant nightmares, then, unable to endure the burden, it falls to Elizabeth, the creature of instinct. And Elizabeth feels things with all of the brute power of a four-year-old human animal. However, having access to Anne's full adult vocabulary, Elizabeth will sometimes panic and go into lengthy speeches to try and persuade the other person to become a safe person, preferably by whatever means I deem befitting.

It's because I feel overwhelmed and helpless. Struggling to get above turbulent water. I need time and space to understand, conceptualize, and explain to myself the way life is. I'm not very good at being a person. So sue me.

Whipped cream.

Andy supported my dream of having two bedrooms. Anne's bedroom would be the one that we shared with Andy, and Elizabeth's room would be the kids' playroom, if we decided to have kids. We had talked it over and decided that one or two kids would be the absolute most. Any more than the replacement rate, and the environmental consequences were monstrous. They were reprehensible as it stood, but that's cognitive dissonance for you. Anyway, then we would each have our own room. Elizabeth's room would be a snug, cozy nest, filled with picture books and stuffed animals. Anne's room would be a haven of dark, many-textured sensuality. Anne's reds and blacks would weave around Andy in the evenings, or else he'd leave Elizabeth to quietly attend to her needs among imaginary worlds, as he traipsed off through his video games, which he'd finally be able to purchase and have at home.

But that was back when there were two adults tucking away for the dream of a mortgage. It was far away, if anywhere. The trailer was right here. The trailer was right now. The trailer was.

In the room in the trailer that Anne and Andy and Elizabeth had shared, there were several stuffed animals. Each had a name, a personality, and an origin story, which I kept in the filing cabinet room, usually accessed through a tunnel at the back of the castle; but there were other ways. Our stuffed animals were a significant part of Andy's and my relationship, appearing in unexpected comical places at Andy's behest, cuddling with us as we watched films and read stories, and helping us to sort out our disagreements.

They were also important councilors to me, the most important outside of the castle grounds. They were with me, usually, when the Davids Bowie read me their books. They were with me, when I was scared, without Andy, and even without Jaimie Taylor. I clutched them in the night.

A baguette.

Anne, Elizabeth said to me one day. She was lawyering. She'd been lawyering all day. She did that a lot, in the time when Jaimie Taylor existed. She even did it to me. She even did it to herself. Anne, she said, Eugene is the only hope of ever having someone to look after us and help us battle monsters.

What about Wolfgang? I said.

Elizabeth went on: He is your doctor. You have seen him maybe eight times, almost always in profession-related circumstances. He sees you as a patient.

I sighed dreamily. We were right. He'd never be interested. He was just another man who'd touched our vagina. He was good at being a doctor; I was good at being a patient. That was all. He was kind, and he was stable, and he was handsome, and he was awkward, and he was funny, and we liked him. But he'd never be interested.

As to Eugene, well, who were we kidding? He'd never taken a shine to us. He had teased Elizabeth from the beginning. And who wants to be a step-parent? Come on, Eileen. (I used to sing that song to myself, with his name in it.)

We were cleaning the Happiness Hotel. Jaimie Taylor was in her baby carrier, mercifully sucking on a pacifier/dragon shield, for once. Duncan Rainbow White tigerishly prowled out from under the bed to our left.

He said, telepathically, the thoughts drifting out of the tips of his gleaming fangs, Annieliz, you need to make a plan for how to take care of yourself for the rest of your life. The one person you know that you're always going to have around is you. Even if Wolfgang or Eugene took up an interest, they might die. Andy did.

Elizabeth and I looked at each other. Elizabeth shrugged.

Eugene doesn't even know that you exist, I pointed out. He only talks to Annieliz because we're always sitting by his fry-cook window. He doesn't know that you're an entity. Plus, he scared you, remember? And he still hasn't said sorry. That's not meeting The Andy Standard.

Elizabeth said, We might could work it out with him, get him to see why he must be more careful.

Anne was getting frustrated with me, I could tell. But she was blinded by the handsomeness and capableness of Wolfgang. Sure, he was smart enough to have become a doctor, but did Wolfgang know how to be a guardian for a little? Was Wolfgang prepared for the intensity of our personality outside of the context of a doctor-patient relationship? I had my doubts. Yes sir, I did.

The creature tapped its pencil on its notepad.

One morning, I sat down on the steps outside of the castle's front door to once again review my options for suicide.

Jaimie Taylor's baby carrier was on the floor between the two beds that I was making, on the second floor of the Happiness Hotel. But it was just a motel in Beckley, West Virginia. It wasn't necessarily happy. Or a hotel.

The garden had grown up into a jungle around the front of the castle. Duncan Rainbow White, in all of his tigerific glory, strolled through the part of the jungle that was by the castle's front steps, where I was sitting, and he said in his low, telepathic roaring color language, You need music.

I put on the song Lazarus, by David Bowie. It was a song on the album that came out right around when he died. I had a Walkman portable cd player with headphones, like the one that Scarlet had back in the nineties. I let the song take me by the tits and dance me away until the beds were made and the bathrooms were scoured and the two dollar tips were collected. I could buy a sandwich at Chez Eloise with that tomorrow, I thought, but it would make more sense to put it toward formula for Jaimie Taylor. I couldn't kill me. I was Annieliz, and Jamie Taylor needed Annieliz. I was better than foster care.

Shredded sharp cheddar, to go in the eggs.

Lots of times, when the castle was still open, and Anne went to work, I'd get to go to the Liza Fronk room! That's the part of the castle where the talking animals are. Once we stopped going into the castle, I had a big sad, but Duncan still came out to play.

We played in the field outside of the castle. The weather in the field tends to be chilly. It's autumn there, and there is something tall and hay-colored instead of grass, lots of that nearby. The field is on the left side of the castle, if you're facing the castle. The same side as the Liza Fronk room. There's a dirt path going up to the castle; Anne and I walk on it from wherever we are for however long it takes until we get to the castle.

Duncan Rainbow White said, You know how your blue might not be my blue, but your blue could be my green?

I said, Yeah.

Duncan smiled his big tiger smile and licked me in the face. What if your giraffes were my killer whales? said Duncan. What if your existential crisis was my pencil sharpener?

I prefer pens to pencils.

The creature added brightly colored gel pens with glitter to its shopping list.

Duncan stretched out, as cats tend to do, with his shiny, almost sparkly, white fur going all aprickle, rainbow stripes flaring up all over as he yawned. His teeth, fangs, tusks, sabers of masticating doom, shone with saliva. He looked at me with a blue-er looking eye, and a blue-but-looked-green eye, with two different sized pupils, like my beloved Bowie, and I knew that he understood, like Andy had understood. He was me. We are them. And Duncan said, What if, since everyone else is gone, you married Eugene?

My Elizabeth-face crinkled in such a way that the crinkles were difficult to undo, like my face was a ball of aluminum foil. Why would we do that? I asked him.

Duncan shook out his fur, with a wooly sound effect. Because taking on a domestic role is a method of disappearing, and visibility is dangerous for you.

We don't need to get married to take on a domestic role, I pointed out.

We sat beneath a tree that wasn't usually there. It showed up by the side of the castle whenever I was with a Liza Fronk animal; the garden also grew itself outside now, much like the garden that had once grown – I wondered if it was growing still – inside of the castle. It was a willow tree. Anne liked willows.

Duncan and the other rainbow animals didn't come outside much. But once Anne got into a regular routine at work, she was always mooning over that Wolfgang Savage, so I started coming here to play, even when Duncan and the raccoon family and the shimmery elephant were gone. I wandered through the field, touching the tip tops of the hay-like stuff. I touched the chilled, damp, grey and brown stones of the castle walls, looking at the pittedness, wondering how and why each little dint and hole came to be. I am full of nothingnesses, Elizabeth thought forlornly, with her four-year-old thoughts.

Duncan Rainbow White appeared at my side again. Eugene is a man of discernment, discipline, dedication, determination, discretion, he said. We could use him on our team. He would be an asset.

I have my doubts about this, Elizabeth replied. He isn't safe. He may be as you said, but he's also a man of criticism, condescension, condemnation, and cruelty. We want his compassion. But we're dealt his cruelty. Cruelty. Remember the incident with the fish? He goes out of his way to say mean things. I think it might be a petty lashing out based on his feelings of inadequacy and lack of power – but the emotional aftermath, even a couple of years later, hasn't felt so petty.

Duncan sang Billy Joel's Innocent Man, quietly, as he strolled away, his tigerish shoulders see-sawing like gladiators bouncing off of the arena floor in rhythmic, buoyant terror, trying to avoid being eaten by the ravenous beasts they were descending into crowds of at intervals, before a bloodthirsty audience of ancient Romans.

A purple monkey, a yellow monkey, and a great green gorilla unfolded themselves from the willow branches, lowered themselves before me, and waited for permission to speak. Go ahead, I told them. The monkeys were almost as large as I was; the great green gorilla was gargantuan compared to me. The purple monkey said, You could become a digital nomad-style bum and travel the world. Or be a tour guide, so that you could work in exotic places.

I don't like talking to people, I said.

The yellow monkey agreed with the purple monkey, though, so I knew it would be good to think it over for a while. The virid gorilla was silent. Gorillas are normally ground-dwelling; he had only been in the tree to consort with the purple monkey with the sapphire eyes and her yellow, but not banana yellow, friend.

Elizabeth objects to bananaish objects. Particularly if they are phallic. I told you I know all of Anne's words. Penis. See. But penis is just an example; penises don't bother me, unless they are wearing banana costumes. Andy's penis sometimes wore a little hat or stocking, but never a yellow one, no siree Bob. I don't mean the Bob like that – I know that your middle name is Robert, but it's an expression, like the ones that they told Mommy in the office would be hard for us to understand.

Duncan looked at me with his David Bowie eyes surrounded by his glimmering white fur, interrupted by pink of neon, blue of neon, orange of neon, and he said to me, You know that Eugene is one of the only ones who can keep up with you in a conversation about evolutionary theories of reality, dragons, particle physics, uncontacted tribes, why there's no such thing as now, Roman history in the context of transgendering, ancient prophesies in the light of block universe theory, black holes, and the sounds that black holes make.

But not the only one, Elizabeth countered. Anne likes Wolfgang. I crossed my arms. And he's a doctor.

Duncan Rainbow White let loose with a Bronx cheer, and rolled his mismatched, perfectly matched, post-punch Bowie eyes.

We were undecided, so we decided to bring the matter back down the dirt path, away from the castle, and into Anne's breakroom office at the hospital in Princeton, West Virginia.

Honey mustard.

One day, Anne and I were walking down the dirt path, and she led us past the castle. We were holding hands. Behind the Castle Bowie was an enormous forest. Anne had Wolfgang Savage on her mind. Ever since we'd stopped going inside the castle, Anne had been thinking a lot about Wolfgang. I wasn't so sure how he'd react to us, if he knew, though. I could picture the look on his face, and the tone in his voice, but I didn't know what would happen to his heart.

Anne said, Elizabeth, I think that Wolfgang would be a great asset. I want him on our team.

We had left our body back at the trailer, playing on the floor with Jaimie Taylor and the glowworm finger puppets, while we watched my Glofriends bootleg dvd on the little portable dvd player that Andy had gotten for us that Christmas.

I said, Anne, are we going to go into the forest? And in we walked. The hollows of some of the trees had books in them. The forest was shadowy, and filled in with every shade of green that I had ever laid eyes on. The leaves shuddered and rippled in a temperamental breeze. Anne picked me up, and carried me to the center of the forest. There was an enormous tree there; I didn't know what kind. Whatever kind we wanted. In its hollow were perfectly fitted shelves, filled with perfectly fitted books. A swing hung on two thick ropes from one thick branch. Anne and I slipped inside of each other sideways, and sat on the swing, to think.

We swung our legs back and forth, pumping, our body rocking, the swing moving us through the rippling green world in a reassuring rhythm, swooping us like Tarzan on a vine, like an astronaut bobbing in space, as slow or as quick or as medium as we liked. We slowed the swing to a standstill in midair, so that we were lying on our back, with our face facing the canopy above us. Sunlight filtered through, warming our skin, drying up tears that we had barely noticed, puddles of our sadness licked up by and absorbed into puddles of light. We exhaled a deep breath, and resumed swinging.

So what if Andy, and Martha, and David Bowie had all died and no longer existed in the world? Andy had never existed in this world, in my world, in the world of my head. But then again, he had only existed there: the things that were Andy externally had interacted with the things that were Annieliz externally, but what did that even mean? An icon on a desktop computer is not the file itself. A brain is not a mind. We hopped down off of the swing, and stepped back out into two bodies. Anne and I sat across from each other, by the tree roots, and played a hand-clapping game.

You know, Anne said, Wolfgang has always treated us respectfully. Not like that Eugene. And Wolfgang is more handsome.

Handsome fades.

We're fading. We're fading right now.

Our appearances were indeed fading into the background green of the forest, the apparitions of our bodies becoming invisible. Soon, the forest was empty. We were gone. The emptiness was pierced by a single cry.

I looked down. Jaimie Taylor was on her back, squalling, as I smiled down at her, making voices with the finger puppets. I sighed.

I got out what was to become the infamous yellow blanket, spread it on the carpet, and spread Jaimie Taylor on it like butter on butter for tummy time, as the pediatrician called it.

I got one of the books off of one of the shelves in the hollow of the tree at the center of the forest of many greens, the forest out behind the Castle Bowie.

The book was How To Care For Your Infant Daughter, by the Thin White Duke. I opened it to page one. On it, written in brilliant, venomous green calligraphy, adorned with vines and tiny animals, medieval style, was a single sentence. It said, Don't have one.

I put the book back, and gazed around the forest. The tree trunks, let alone the tree branches, were bending and swaying, thick trunks, trunks that had withstood storms, trunks that hadn't moved ever, not since they'd grown there, not since the wind had blown their sapling bodies. Everything was changing. The ground moved vaguely, slightly, beneath our feet. It wasn't quite like an earthquake. A little like if a sandbox were covered over with fabric, then tilted mildly from side to side and diagonally and back and forth and all over as you tried to walk across it. Not undoable, just

uncomfortable, a ground you couldn't get used to walking on,
because could you even call that thing a ground anymore? It looked
like a ground. But it was wiggly. You couldn't be sure of your next
step, not in any direction, and you couldn't be sure of standing still
either. I looked up, but the faltering forest canopy made me feel
dizzy, so I looked around at my aroundnesses instead.

Anne said, Elizabeth, are you seeing what I'm seeing?

And I said, Maybe you should check on the baby, so she did,
and when she got back, she told me, She's just lying there,
touching those plastic things. Elizabeth, are you seeing what I'm
seeing?

I said, Well that depends. I'm seeing a thing that was a forest a
minute ago, or at least a pretty good idea of a forest, but now it isn't
acting like a forest. It's because you had a baby. It's an
unpredictable force. I told you.

When did you tell me? Anne blurted, drawing her chin back.

Back when we lived in the blue A-frame house, before they
ruined it, and we were playing school, and I told you how bad it was

going to be to try to figure out how to discipline a kid and feed it every day. Now we can barely feed us, I said, throwing my hands in a big arch. No matter how far I threw them, though, they were always still at the ends of my arms.

The greens all around us had become more distinct, more individual. Anne's hair looked dark, a special kind of dark, though I could see that it was no darker than usual. You need a nap, I told her.

Anne said, I nap when the baby naps.

Jaimie Taylor never sleeps for more than twenty-eight minutes at a time, I tried to tell her. You couldn't reason with Anne; she was an adult. Jaimie Taylor is a baby. You are a grown-up, and grown-ups cannot function acceptably on only naps. Naps that only last less than half an hour, too! Honestly, look at this place! It's a disaster!

Outside the edges of the slow-hula-dancing thick strong tree trunks, I could just see the beginnings of the trailer's living room, the trailer's stomach, where there should have been more forest.

Life is all out of place, Anne.

Nonesense, Elizabeth. We're in a stable place right now. I have my job in the human resources department, and the Happiness Hotel, plus the extra income from walking Dr. Hanging's dogs. The trailer is paid off, so we can afford almost everything we need on ten dollars an hour.

Everything WE need, but Jaimie Taylor isn't like us! She's going to get bigger. She's going to need more and more food, more and more clothing, and if she's going to keep up with the world and have anything like a normal social development – which she will need to function as an adult, because you made a future adult, let's not forget that – she's going to, in that sense, need electronics.

You're getting ahead of yourself, Anne said, placing her hands on my shoulders. Jamie Taylor is just a baby. We don't know what this situation is going to be in ten years.

Well, according to Eliezer Yudkowski –

Anne held her hand up. She knew that I was about to bring up an illustration from Harry Potter and the Methods of Rationality, she knew because she was me, because her brain had thought it in my head, but by now, the forest had begun melting. Except when you looked right at it. Then the greens would sharpen up again. The trees had ceased to slow-hula. Everything had ceased except for a low, baroomfing hum. I could sense a slow brown monster, its fur all furry, round and huge and lumbering right at us! Run!

But our body wasn't running. It was sitting on the floor of our paid-off-because-it-was-inherited-from-a-dead-old-woman trailer, making educational baby talk at a baby that had been made partially by Andy, who was also dead.

Hot chocolate with extra marshmallows! We just ran out.

A couple of moons ago, Wolfgang Savage popped by the trailer unannounced. He was only standing on half a foot at a time. He looked at the plastic dinosaur scene in the plant beside the screen door. He looked at Annieliz, through the grey filter. Her eyes were wide, her mouth rounded with surprise.

I tactlessly blurted, What are you doing here?

Between the fingertips of both hands, barely touched by any one bit of him at once, he held a business-sized envelope. He handed it to me.

I wanted to deliver this personally, because there has been such a mix-up with paperwork at the hospital during the renovation, for some reason. This was delivered to Andy's work mailbox, but it should have gotten to you weeks ago.

I looked at the envelope. It was from Hawthorne Bros. Insurance. I looked at Wolfgang Savage's face. It was from West Virginia.

Open it, Annieliz, he urged. You won't want that getting lost in the scuffle.

He didn't appear to be looking into the disaster area of a trailer behind my shoulders, but I was still in the process of sorting through Jaimie Taylor's baby things, which I was preparing to donate. Even the expensive crib. There would be no more children.

My fingers slowly tore apart the envelope, extracted the letter, and held it up to me. Anne read without much interest, expecting nonsense, a bill, a late fee.

It was a letter telling me about claims I'd need to file, detailing a life insurance payout for Andy, and a life insurance payout for Jaimie Taylor. I hadn't even known there was a policy.

I handed the letter to Wolfgang in unblinking silence.

Come inside, I said, not waiting for him to finish reading.

He followed me. We sat at the kitchen table, which was technically the hallway table, as there was no room in what passed for our actual kitchen. There were papers piled high, mostly my loose sketches and journals.

Dr. Savage set the letter down and touched my eyes with his from a distance. Annieliz, this is a lot of money, he said. You need to talk to a lawyer, or an investor, or something.

Andy's mother must have called them, I muttered. I didn't even know we had life insurance.

Wolfgang nodded. Do you want me to walk you through this? I don't want to condescend. Just knowing you've been through a lot lately, and.

Yes, I suppose I'll need to go to the library, so I can use the computer. Would you like some hot chocolate? I don't have any coffee.

The creature gazed down at its list, flaring its nostrils.

As the things that Andy had planned for came together, I made a ten-year plan.

First thing was, call Scarlet, to check on her butt.

Next order of business: gage Eloise's interest in participating. She would decline, I knew; Eloise had the diner to take care of; she had a life here. Adventures would come to her when she called them. Not before.

Being a logical, down to earth person, I was able to set aside my dreams of Wolfgang, knowing that they'd only ever been dreams anyway. He was way out of our league. It would not occur to him to consider dating us. I would dream on, but I couldn't hang around, waiting to see if dreams would come true.

Elizabeth was curled in a ball, crying from terror as I made the lists: what to donate, what to buy, what to throw out, what to pack. And finally, this last one: a grocery list, for my remaining time at home.

Elizabeth was loathe to give up the idea of Eugene; no matter how often I reminded her of the way he took out his insecurities on other people in the form of rude, hostile arrogance. No matter how plainly I laid before her her own insistent arguments that Eugene was mean and scary, she clung to the idea, convinced that he would make a good guardian to her little. I explained that Wolfgang would probably also be an excellent caretaker, but she wanted evidence.

But since neither man was interested in us, and never would be, it hardly mattered. We were on our own, as we always had been, except for those few years with Andy.

You're nearly caught up now. Don't think I hadn't questioned it – why from childhood had I conceptualized myself as a white man; why did I fixate steadfastly on men who would never reciprocate interest; why was I reluctant to take care of me, despite the fact that I was capable? Perhaps I was trying to make up for something, to fix what had happened in the banana room, to distract me from the creature I'd become. Duncan Rainbow White shrugged his shiny shoulders. We were sitting on the mossy, overgrown castle steps. I didn't know what to do. Elizabeth was pouting, which hurt me physically – I could feel her tension in my chest, her bitterness in my heart.

The cheese stands alone. We'd stay single for life, and travel around the world. We'd do it cheaply, discreetly, using our hospitality degree and experience to work in youth hostels and bed and breakfasts the world over, never staying in one place for more than a couple of months at a time, like those solo travelers on reddit. We'd work on organic farms, homesteads, building projects, in exchange for food and shelter, to make the money stretch as long as possible. We needn't plan too far ahead, as the cyst forking our cerebellum might rupture at any time, ending us once and for all. But until then, we were alone, and we would wander. That much,

Elizabeth could be excited about. She'd always wanted us to roam about the globe.

Suddenly, she bolted off of my lap, running the remaining second between me and there, at the heavy, imposing, brown-with-black-metal-trim wooden front door of the castle.

Elizabeth knocked.

And there you were. There you were, Mr. David Robert Jones, the Last and Elder Bowie, and behind you, seven thrones, and six grins spreading across six faces. And the first one said, You remind me of the

Author's Note

Connor Grail lyrics used by permission.

www.ingramcontent.com/pod-product-compliance
Lightning Source LLC
Chambersburg PA
CBHW021147130626
46554CB00005B/1699